REDSTORY

The Story of Red

Library of Congress Catalog Card
Number: TXu 1-826-597
ISBN: 978-0-9891727-0-7

Redstory
(The story of Red)
Alethea's narrative

by,

D Alexander Griffin

CONTENTS

Chapter I

The Visit

The night was dark and rainy. At times, one could see the moon creep through the clouds and then it would vanish as if it was never there. The wind was blowing fiercely and fallen tree limbs were scattered around the houses on the block and in the street. Out of the shadows emerged a figure moving with the speed of a gazelle and the agility of a panther. The figure closes in on one of the neighborhood houses. There is a faint light coming from the second floor window. Like a spider, the figure scales the south wall of the house and closes in on the small window. He slowly pushes the window open and steps into the semi-darkened room. As the window opens a figure appears out of the shadows. The clouds separate for a moment and as the moonlight shines into the window, the figure appears to be the silhouette of a man. He's wearing a hat, tipped low over his forehead, and he's dressed in a perfectly tailored black suit. He's now standing perfectly still. Also in the room is a baby that should be fast asleep at this hour but for some reason is wide awake. The baby is not crying, just sitting up in his crib as if he is waiting for something. The baby watches the man closely; fixated on his every move. The baby has a peculiar red skin that seems to glow in the dimly lit room. The baby's facial features are more chiseled than soft and his eyes are black like onyx. The man moves closer to the crib and stands over the baby. The child gazes up and stares at the man as if he knew who he was. This beautiful baby boy is not yet a year old but he has the motor skills of a child much older. The child promptly sits up as if to formally address his visitor.

The man tips his hat up so that the child can see a portion of his face. He, too, has red skin. The man's name is Hezekiah and although his age is not apparent by looking at him, he carries himself like a man of many years. The man starts to speak in a strong yet soft voice.
"My brother, you will come to know that you are vastly different from others, Hezekiah said." "You are special and have a significant part to play in this world's future. Our brotherhood has continued to evolve and your generation will be the one that makes the final steps to capturing our destiny. You will be a leader of men in every stage of your life. You will one day understand your purpose in life. One day, you will embrace your destiny! Our race will unify and take..."

Hezekiah stops speaking abruptly. His ears twitch. He hears footsteps from the hall outside the door of the room. He steps quickly back to the window, faster than it would seem humanly possible. When he reaches the window ledge, he looks back at the baby who has turned to watch Hezekiah's every move. Hezekiah makes one last statement.

"See you soon my brother!"

In one quick move Hezekiah leaps out of the window and vanishes into the night. Just as he leaves, a young woman opens the door and enters the room. Her movements are urgent and fretful. Could she have heard a man's voice coming from her child's room? Instead, she finds her beautiful child sitting up, wide awake, but alone. The baby raises his arms; she can see from his gestures that he is thirsty, not likely for milk, but for water. Ever since he was born her child preferred to drink water instead of milk. She lifts him from his crib, carries him downstairs to the kitchen and gives him a baby's bottle, filled with water. The baby drinks the water, quickly and thirstily, as if he had not had a drink for weeks. She chuckles softly, amazed that her son can drink so much water, yet rarely has a wet diaper. "Where does all that water go," she wonders to herself. After his thirst is quenched, she takes her son back upstairs and tucks him under the covers and softly and lovingly pats his bottom. Turning to leave the room, she notices that the window is slightly ajar. As she moves across the room to close the window, she sees a small puddle of water on the floor under the window sill. It had been raining hard all evening, but given that the window was sheltered by a low-hanging awning, she was surprised that so much water had come inside the window.

Finding a small towel lying on the dresser nearby, she kneels down and dries the floor. As she closes the window, and turns back toward her baby's crib, she sees that her beautiful boy is already fast asleep. She leans over him, kisses his forehead and turns toward the bedroom door to leave.

"Sweet dreams Dane," she whispers, as she closes the door. "I love you."

Chapter II

Cruise

Harris hadn't had a vacation in over two years and he was really looking forward to this one. He so enjoyed cruise vacations because once the ship left the loading dock, he could completely relax. He wouldn't need to drive anywhere, he didn't have to cook, he didn't even have to plan his social activities. The cruise staff would take care of everything for him. He had never been on a cruise on the Aegean Sea and he had always wanted to see the islands around Turkey. He had dreamed of taking his next vacation in a warm climate and he knew he wanted to be surrounded by water. He convinced his friends, Charles, Patrick, Toni and Stacy, that they, too, needed to take some time off and that taking a cruise together would be a fabulous adventure for them.

Now Harris, his friends and hundreds of vacationers gathered around the loading dock waiting to board the massive Ocean liner. The ship had five levels of spacious quarters for passengers. There were ten swimming pools, two casinos, seven full-service restaurants and five specialty food spots. Passengers could exercise in any of the three gyms, which were equipped with treadmills, elliptical machines, free weights and several rooms for yoga and pilates classes. Passengers could spend their days at sea strolling through either of the two tree-lined parks; they could toss Frisbees, or play touch football on the grassy fields. Every amenity imaginable was available for passengers. It was just like a small resort town floating on water.

By the time the ship was just a few miles from the docks and heading toward the open sea, Harris was at peace. No phones, no Internet, just the most beautiful sound he has ever heard -- the sound of the ocean. Harris sat for hours on the deck, breathing in the cool, salt-filled air and enjoying every moment. He had gone on vacations with his friends in the past and he loved that they could have so much fun together – hiking, biking and exploring the cultural sites of the cities and towns they visited. But this time, when the ship docked and his friends rushed ashore to take in the local culture; Harris was perfectly content staying behind on the ship. He usually spent his mornings near one of the ship's ten swimming pools. It wasn't because he liked to watch women in bikinis or sunbath. In fact, he didn't really like the sun much at all. His skin was a beautiful red color but in the sun his skin would dry out and quickly turn pale. And even though he would constantly slather on sunscreen, it would seemingly evaporate off his skin as soon as he thought he was suitably covered with it. No... Harris just wanted to be near or in water.

Although the Aegean Sea is normally quite calm in comparison to the Atlantic and Pacific oceans, this year, the Sea had been uncommonly turbulent. Even given the massive size of the ship, many of the ship's passengers had already succumbed to motion-sickness by the second day of the cruise. Harris' friends were just miserable, but he was just fine. In fact, the more the ship rocked, the more at ease Harris felt. After the third day of unseasonable weather and rocky seas, the ship's crew decided to dock near a small island. Harris' friends were elated, relieved and eager to step on solid ground again. Harris would have loved to have stayed on the ship, but since he had invited his friends to join him on this cruise, Harris didn't want them to feel like he didn't want to spend time with them. Besides, his friends loved going on vacation with Harris because he spoke several languages and could communicate with just about anyone. Harris had been studying hard to learn enough of the Turkish language that he could get around with not problem.   Harris' friends had hoped that he would be able to assist them in negotiating with shopkeepers, help with picking meals at local restaurants and ultimately ensuring that their vacation travel experience would be authentic.

So they all went ashore and were quickly engaged in their normal adventures, checking out the sights and buying trinkets, hats, rugs, t-shirts and tote bags – items they would never use once they got back home, but which seemed like good purchases if only because they were on vacation and could splurge a bit.

In the evenings, Harris liked to sit out on the deck of the ship to clear his mind. This was the best part of his vacations. In the quiet and peacefulness of the evening, he could dream and craft ideas that would help him in life back on shore. It was during a cruise like this one, three years ago, when he came up with the idea for a new product that had saved his company millions of dollars. In fact, it seemed that every time he returned from his cruise vacations, he would ultimately get a raise at work because his ideas, when implemented, kept his company ahead of the competition. He had proven many times that he was the smartest, most innovative person in the company. The senior management team had identified him as an invaluable contributor to the company's success. He had been identified and placed on the fast track for leaders within the company. Harris believed that it would only be a few more years before he was running the company as its chief executive officer.

But for some reason, this vacation was different. The ideas weren't flowing as easily. He was restless, he couldn't sleep and he felt drawn to spending every moment out on the deck, close to the water. On the fifth night of the cruise, events took place that would change his life forever.

As Harris was making his customary walk around the deck at 2:00 am he noticed a group of people drinking and hanging out near the edge of the boat. Harris thought they were college students and, because of the time of year, they were most likely on Spring

Break. One guy from the group was attempting to stand up and walk on the ship's railing despite the signs posted along the deck that warned passengers to keep off the railings. The drunken student jumped on the railing and convinced his friends to join him in his antics. Harris quickly stood by and watched as a few of them were able to climb onto the top railing and successfully walk about twenty feet on the railing. A young woman from the group climbed up on the railing and attempted to join her friends, but she was noticeably tipsy and was having trouble balancing. Then the unthinkable happened. The young woman lost her balance, slipped from the top of the railing, and fell five stories into the ocean.

As Harris watched in horror as the young woman fell into the ocean, something came over him, something he had never experienced before in his life. He had a compelling urge to jump over the side after her. Her drunken friends immediately became more alert and started screaming for help. Several of the ship's crew members started running towards the group, trying to determine the cause for the alarm. Harris started running at full speed towards the ship's railing where the young woman had fallen into the ocean. He leaped through the air touched the ledge with one foot and catapulted himself down towards the water. He plummeted at a speed he had never before experienced. As his body approached the surface of the water, he felt in total control. He extended his body into a straight line just as an Olympic diver would.

He plunged into the ocean and was immediately surrounded by darkness. Yet in the cold, turbulent waters, Harris found that he could see around him quick clearly. Beneath the surface, the ocean was as clear as if it was day. He quickly scanned his surroundings, looking for the young woman. He finally saw her. She was about fifty feet beneath him and she was sinking fast. He started swimming, descending towards her, moving through the water as swiftly and quickly as a shark would as it approached its prey. It was as if he was flying through the water. With just a few easy kicks of his feet, he was right next to her. He reached out for her, grabbed her and within seconds he was heading back to the ocean's surface. He felt like a bird in flight even though he was swimming underwater. When he reached the ocean's surface, he swam toward a life buoy that one of the ship's crew members had thrown into the water near the place that the woman had fallen in the water. Harris tied the rope on the body of the semi-conscious woman and watched as ship's attendants lifted her the deck.

The waves were huge and relentlessly crashing against the side of the ship. Harris tried to
keep his head above water and every time he
made his way to the surface, another wave
would furiously crash down on him. Yet Harris was not frightened at all. Surely the
woman would not have survived for much
longer in the open water. But he was at peace.
He was in control in the water in a way that
he had never experienced on land. The ship's
attendants threw another life buoy into the
water for him, but because the surface of the
water was so agitated, the buoy kept moving
farther and farther away from him. Again and
again, he tried swimming towards the buoy,
but the strong current kept pushing it away
from him. Then almost instinctively, he decided to try swimming underwater toward the
buoy.

By then a large crowd had gathered on the

deck of the ship, trying to determine what just happened. Several of the passengers and the ship's attendants started looking across the surface of the water for Harris. No one had spotted him in the last ten minutes and they were all fearful that he had drowned.

Harris knew he had been under water for a long time and wondered how long he could hold his breath before he would have to surface. As he descended deep beneath the surface of the sea, he felt his chest moving in and out as if he was breathing. But he knew this couldn't be the case since he was at least fifteen feet under water. In fact, Harris didn't even feel the urge to breath. He didn't feel the need to struggle. He was comfortable, as if he belonged in the sea.

Harris started swimming towards the lights of the ship that were reflected even in the depths of the sea. He started yelling for help, but the ship's attendants couldn't hear him. They couldn't hear him because he was still under the surface. But how could he be yelling under water? As he approached the surface, he spotted the buoy, swam toward it, grabbed it and put it under his arms. He immediately started to feel a strong tug as the ship's attendant worked to pull him out of the sea.

When he reached the deck, he noticed the ship's paramedics hovering over the young woman that he had saved. The woman was exhausted, completely spent and she had taken in a lot of water, but Harris had a feeling that she would survive. He had rescued her in the nick of time. As Harris was gazing at the woman, she caught his eye and gave him a look that expressed her gratitude. She mustered up the strength to mouth the words 'thank you."

Some of the passengers started cheering when they saw Harris. Some were crying tears of joy and relief. Harris could feel their gratitude. He was a hero. A few of the para- medics rushed toward him and asked him to sit down so they could examine him. Harris did not feel the need to sit. He had so much adrenaline running through his veins that he was definitely more comfortable standing. They offered him oxygen, but he didn't need it. They tried to throw blankets over his shoulders to warm him and dry him off, but Harris enjoyed the moisture from the sea on his skin. It was like the refreshing feel of a moisturizing body lotion and he didn't want them to rub it off.

Harris assured the paramedics that he was alright and he started to make his way through the crown of onlookers. Everyone wanted to shake his hand or pat him on the back for rescuing the young woman. Also, in the crowd were two men dressed in suits that approached Harris. They introduced themselves as the ship's police and said they wanted to ask him a few questions. Harris politely declined and told them that he just wanted to go back to his room to try and relax. The two men insisted that Harris just answer a few questions. Harris, now a bit perturbed, adamantly said "not tonight!" and walked away. As he made his way through the ship's corridors, his mind went back to the events of the evening, from the time he jumped into the water to save the young woman to being pulled from the water by the ship's attendants. So many questions began to run through his mind, questions that he ultimately could not answer. After spending so much time in the water, why didn't he feel cold? How was he able to find the woman so quickly in the dark and turbulent waters? And the biggest question was, how had he been able to stay under water for so long without oxygen?

Chapter III

Others Like Us

Matthew had lived most of his eleven years in a small town in the Pacific Northwest never having met anyone like him in person. He had never met anyone who had red skin like his that radiated in the sun and shined bright in the rain. There were many prominent people like him he would see on television like; businessmen, senators, professional athletes, musicians and even the Vice President of the United States. Matthew had seen a couple of kids at the his high school who were like him, but always from a distance, never close enough for him to get a good look or to touch them. The kids who were like him were active in sports and Matthew always felt compelled to root for them, even though he didn't know them or had ever come within a hundred yards of them.

Matthew's parents were not like him at all. They had pale skin without much color. He often overheard his parents talking late at night, wondering out loud how they could have ever conceived someone like him. Matthew knew his parents loved him. Over the years, they had always supported him in every way. He knew he could count on them and that they would do anything for him. He also knew they were often ridiculed by their colleagues at work, just as he was ridiculed by his schoolmates.

One day, as Matthew was taking a walk in his neighborhood, he saw a kid about the same age as he was. The kid's skin was a beautiful shade of red. As they approached each other, they both stopped and stared at each other. It was as if they both have seen a ghost. In reality, neither of them had ever seen someone like themselves up-close. As they awkwardly and silently stared at each other, it seemed as if minutes were passing, but it was probably just seconds.

Then, Matthew finally heard something very comforting. It was a friendly greeting.

"Hi, how are you?" The other boy asked with a smile.

"I'm fine, and you?" Matthew responded.

"I'm good."

"My name is Matthew, but most people call me Matt."

"My name is Sanjay," the other boy said proudly.

"Do you live around here?" Matthew asked.

Matthew knew the answer before he posed the question to Sanjay. He had lived in that town his entire life and had always longed to meet someone like him. The town was so small that he was sure if there was someone like him in his neighborhood, he would have known.

"No, I just moved here from the New Mexico," said Sanjay.

"New Mexico is a long way away from Washington." Matthew said. "Did your parents move here because of a job?"

"Yes partly, but also because the desert environment was so harsh on my skin. It caused me to have severe cases of eczema. My doctor told them that I needed a change of climate."

"Your skin looks fine to me."

"Thanks. We have been here two weeks now and every day that it rains, my skin gets better. I really feel alive when it rains. I like to go outside more when it's raining than when it's sunny. I feel stronger and more confident when I'm in the rain."

"Me too!" Matthew said. He could barely contain his excitement. "I feel the same way when it rains. Is that weird?"

"Not anymore weirder than our red skin, Sanjay says."

(They both laugh heartily)

"So do you know anyone else with red skin?" Matthew asked.

"Yes. There was an older gentleman at my church that had the same skin. I talked to him all the time about random subjects. He was very kind to me, I guess probably because our skin was the same color and he knew what I must have been was going through."

"Do either of your parents have red skin?"

Matthew asked.

"No." "No one in my family has red skin," Sanjay said. "Yours?"

"No," Matthew said sadly.

Sanjay then asked, "Do you feel alone sometimes?"

"All of the time," Matthew replied. "I know my parents love me and I have friends that like me, but most people seem to have a problem with my appearance. I know it's because they think there is something wrong with me. I wish there were more people like us around here. Then we wouldn't stand out so much."

"I can't say that I don't wish the same thing sometimes, because I do," Sanjay said. "My father told me that I was special and that I had gifts that the other kids didn't have. When I asked my father what those gifts were, he said it should be obvious. At the time, however, I didn't understand what he meant. He said most kids would give anything to be as smart and athletic as I was. He told me that I should never try to blend in because that would make me average and why be average when you can be so much more? He always encourages me to continue to learn more and practice harder. He said the benefits may not be obvious now, but they will be in the future."

Matthew thought those seemed like words of wisdom. Clearly, Sanjay had a different perspective on life. He seemed to be more comfortable being different from everyone. In Sanjay's eyes, his differences were positive attributes. Sanjay wanted to have friends, to be accepted, but not at the expense of compromising who he was. Matthew thought it was refreshing to hear this way of thinking.

Then, Matthew noticed something rather peculiar. He was communicating with Sanjay in

a way that was different than his normal conversations. In fact, Matthew couldn't really
remember if he was hearing their conversation with his ears or if he was just imagining
that they were talking. It was as if Sanjay and
he were communicating telepathically. By the
way Sanjay was looking at him; it seemed as
if they both had come to this realization at
the same time.

Chapter IV

High School Crush

Emma entered the kitchen with her hair in neat braids. She was wearing a fitted short sleeve shirt with the name of her school and logo across the chest. The skirt she was wearing was a tad bit short. Emma's mother was sitting at the kitchen table, holding a cup of coffee and reading the *Living* section of the Sunday paper. Emma's father was also sitting at the table. He was wearing his favorite sweats and reading the *Sports* section of the paper. As Emma walked toward the sink, her mother looked over the top of the paper. She sees Emma and starts grinning from ear to ear.

"Who is this boy you are all 'goo goo' about?" Emma's mother asks.

"Mom, I'm not 'goo goo'," Emma says with an embarrassing look on her face.

"That's what your mouth says, but I've known you for your whole life, and I know there is more to the story. Tell me something about him."

"He is just a boy from school."

"Okay, what is he like," Emma's mom asks, even more intrigued.

"He's like, cool," Emma says with a bit more confidence.

Emma's father jumps in the conversation. "What does that mean? Does he play sports?"

"Yes, he's on the swim team, the basketball team and the football team." Emma says, knowing this would make her father instantly like him.

"Is he any good?" Emma's father asks, suddenly taking more of an interest in the conversation.

"He's starting on the basketball team and scores a lot of points."

"Nice. What position does he play on the football team?" Emma's father asks.

Emma's father played football in high school, so Emma knew this would be the next questions her father would ask.

"I'm not sure I know," Emma replied. "I just know that he yells at the team and throws the ball a lot."

"So is he a quarterback?" her father says as he leans back in his chair with a proud look on his face.

"I think so." Emma said, knowing she really should know what position her boyfriend played.

"So he is the quarterback on the football team

and he scores a lot of points on the basketball team." Emma's father says. " I suppose he is also good at swimming?"

"Yes, I don't think he has lost a competition," Emma replied.

"Wow, he hasn't lost a competition this year?" Emma's mother says with amazement.

"I don't think he has ever lost a competition, Emma says."

"Well, this kid sounds like a winner." Emma's mother says. Then she asks the question that Emma knows she's been waiting to ask.

"Is he smart?"

"Well, I met him in my Math AP class. He is often able to answer questions even the teacher can't answer."

Now Emma's mother has a proud look on her face.

"So when do we get to meet this boy?"

Emma's mother asks.

"Why do you want to meet him?" Emma says uneasily.

Emma's father speaks, "Well, to check him out, to see if he's alright to be hanging out with my daughter."

"Well, I don't think we are ready for that." Emma says.

"Why not?" Emma's mother asks, now looking a bit concerned.

"We are just not that serious yet." Emma adds.

"Well, we don't have to meet him formally." Emma's mother says to ease the conversation. I just want to see who his is. Isn't there a football game this weekend?"

"Yes, but I'll be going with my friends."

"Okay," her mother says, "but what does that mean?"

"It's not cool to have your parents at the game. The other kids will laugh at me!"

Emma exclaims.

Emma's father jumps back in the conversation. "What about the parents who have kids playing in the game?"

"That's different," Emma says.

"Why?" Emma's mother asks.

"Because those parents have a legitimate reason to be there."

"What if I just want to see a high school game?" Emma's father asks.

"No one wants to do that," says Emma.

"Well, I went to your school and played quarterback on the football team," her father says proudly.

"That was in the stone ages," Emma said.

"Did they play under the lights or candles?"

"That's pretty funny young lady." Her father replies.

(They all laugh)

What they didn't know was that Emma's boyfriend was not like other guys. He was more than just an athlete who was smart. His talents were extraordinary, unlike any other student who had attended that school. His name was Tomlin.

Chapter V

Sneaker Waves

As Dorian stepped outside of his beach house, he noticed something different. This specific morning, the ocean was extremely subdued. The light in the sky was still faint, but the sun was rising at a seemingly frantic pace. The wind was so low and quiet that the only air he could hear moving around him was his own breath. The sound of the waves was faint in his ears, yet Dorian was aware of the surf's continuous rhythmic beat. The sand was still cool from the night before. The salty air was so fresh and poignant that it dominated his sense of smell. He could almost taste the air. As Dorian's eyes gazed towards the sunrise, there was, as far as he could see, a never-ending ocean. The bluish green color of the water gradually darkened as his eyes approached the horizon. A group of sea gulls were flying in a circle in the distance, surely scouting for fish just beneath the surface of the water. The scenery resembled a picture of paradise, like a piece of artwork in a galley. It was almost as if it was not real. Dorian thanked God everyday for blessing him with such beautiful scenery.

No sound could be heard from the row of houses that lined the beach. The residents had not yet opened their blinds or windows to usher in the fresh morning air. And, at this hour, the shops and offices were still closed, except for the twenty-four hour convenience store on the corner.

At an early age, Dorian learned to never turn

his back on the ocean. His mother, Anya, would often tell him stories about sneaker waves that would seemingly come out of no-where. These waves would snatch anything in its path and draw it out to the ocean. Dorian imagined that these waves were like a giant vacuum that could suck an adult man fifteen miles from the shore before dumping him in the bottom of the ocean.

Dorian had just turned forty years old and was still an exceptional athlete. He was just over six-feet tall with a lean and slender build. He walked with a rhythm that exuber-ated a quiet confidence. His skin was a warm burgundy color that looked brown from a dis-tance.

Dorian was never afraid of the water despite the stories his mother told him. In fact, even though he was not a great swimmer, when-

ever he was near a large body of water, he felt
safe. There was something about water that
really energized him.

Yet Dorian was always perplexed about his
affinity to water especially since he had almost drowned when he was a child. He remembers that day as if it were yesterday. He
was on vacation with his family and they all
wanted to go to the pool for a swim. Dorian's
father was a decent swimmer and his mother
was not a strong swimmer, but she was comfortable in the water. Dorian was sitting on
the edge of the pool while all of the adults
were swimming or talking amongst themselves in the water. The pool didn't have a
section for kids and the shallowest end of the
pool was four feet. Dorian wasn't quite four
feet tall yet so his parents told him to just sit
on the edge of the pool with his feet in the
water. Eventually Dorian became bored with

just sitting on the edge. He wanted to play. He at least wanted to stick his feet farther into the water. So he started with one leg and slid it further into the water. This was amusing to him so he decided to do the same with the other leg. As he shifted his body position to stick the other leg in further, he lost his balance and slipped completely under the water. Because he slid in, there was no splash. No one saw or heard him enter the water.

He tried to swim as he had seen other people swim. He started reaching up and forward with his arms and pulling them back to his sides, while furiously kicking his legs. But with all of this effort, he was not making any progress. He could see the surface of the water, but could not get there and he knew he could only hold his breath for a limited amount of time. The more he tried to swim faster, the more he realized he wasn't moving closer to the surface. He felt like he couldn't hold his breath anymore and took in a huge gasp. Right then, his father grabbed his arm and pulled him out of the water. Despite being traumatized by the experience, Dorian remembers that he didn't even cough when he was pulled out. He did not know how long he was under water but it felt like an eternity. He wondered how he could have been under water for so long and not have drowned. The other thing that he couldn't figure out was how he had gasped for air under water yet he hadn't taken any water into his lungs?

Years later he still thinks about that day, not because of the fear he felt, but because he felt so alive afterwards. He felt as if God was looking after him.

After having such a traumatic experience as a child, most people would be scared to go near the water. But not Dorian. He had heard others talking about people being drawn to water, how the oceans seems to call a person. Well, Dorian *could* actually hear voices coming from the water. These voices were friendly, inviting and made him feel at ease which is why he loved walking on the beach, and gazing out over the ocean. He had decided to study marine biology in college because he wanted to spend his career and for that matter his life around water.

As Dorian was walking on the beach as he always did early in the morning, a feeling of fear that he thought he'd never experience, suddenly came upon him. Just then, a sneaker wave came out of nowhere and crashed down on him knocking him to the sand. The wave quickly and forcefully receded back out to the ocean and took Dorian with it. Suddenly, everything was dark around him. He could sense that he was tumbling around and around. He bumped into something hard but it didn't stop him. He kept tumbling and tumbling and he knew he was being carried out to the ocean.

Dorian had tried to stay as calm as possible. He felt he had been holding his breath for more than five minutes. He remarkably felt like he could hold it as long as it took for him to stop tumbling. As he started to slow down, he opened his eyes wide to get an assessment on where he may have ended up. It was pitch black, but he could see the silhouettes of objects. It was quiet all around him, but he thought he could hear rhythmic noises that sounded like people in conversation.

The environment had a weird feel to it. It was one he couldn't put his finger on but it was familiar. He could feel sand between his toes as if he was still standing on the beach. Then he realized he was on the ocean floor. The thought of that was frightening but what was even scarier for him to imagine was how far he had gone away from shore. He thought, how deep under water was he? His body ached from all of the tumbling. He felt weary as if he had been a passenger in multiple car wrecks. All of these things should have caused Dorian to experience extreme panic, but he was surprisingly calm.

Then, a few things ran though his mind that he would not be able to answer. First, how could he have held his breath for so long? Secondly, how come the weight of the water and the strength of the wave had not ripped him to shreds. Thirdly, what were all the voices he was hearing around him. And finally, how could he now be breathing heavily from exhaustion, underwater?

Chapter VI

Board Room

The board room was on the forty-first floor and was surrounded by windows. The view was incredible. The sky was a rich blue and there were a few nimbus clouds scattered around but not enough to block the rays of the sun. In the middle of the board room was a large table that could seat about twenty people. This table was "state of the art" with multiple power plugs for computes and Wi-Fi access for the internet. The chairs in the room were large, comfortable and equipped with several ergonomic settings. In one corner of the board room was a small table with pitch-ers of water, canisters of coffee, soda and a few pastries. Sunlight filled the room and created a glare but because it was late fall, and the middle of the rainy season, no one wanted to close the blinds. Knowing that it would be another three months of clouds, everyone wanted to soak up as much sun as possible. The meeting attendees were all dressed in suits and normally they were quite a boisterous group when they got together. This day however, the room was quiet. There were no side conversations; no one was multitasking on their laptops or smart phones.

"We all know that global warming is real," says Reed. "It's obvious. For an example closer to home, take a look at the drastic temperature changes in all regions of the US." "We have been talking about global warming for the past forty years and we are no closer to having a hole in the ozone than we were then," Paul counters. "We need to keep mining the earth for resources. Our global economy is dependent on it."

Reed sat more erectly in his chair. His frustration showed on his face. "There won't be a global economy if we don't do anything about global warming!" Reed exclaims. "We have a responsibility to our children to make some adjustments now to try and preserve the luxuries we have like fresh water, fresh air..."

"There is nothing to worry about. We have made some concessions in the way we work. We have done enough." Paul says equally frustrated.

"What happens when things really start to directly affect our society?" Reed continues.

"Like the fact that we have red people?" Paul says with a smirk."

"I am not going to acknowledge that statement," Reed says, glaring at Paul.

Reed was a tall, slender man with skin the color of blood. He had striking features and eyes that peered through you as if he could look into your soul.

Paul goes on. "Why not? Forty years ago I don't remember seeing any red people. Now they are everywhere."

"Races don't just start up overnight; nor does racism." Reed says, looking directly at Paul.

"Are you calling me a racist?" says Paul, visibly angry, pointing a finger at Reed.

"Are you calling me a freak of nature?" Reed replies sharply.

"Yes, I am. There is nothing natural about someone with red skin." says Paul.

"Then yes, I am calling you a racist," Reed retorts.

Seeing that tempers are about to explode. Randal interrupts the conversation.

"Gentlemen, we are not here to have this conversation." Randal says sternly. "We are here to determine what steps we can take to keep socicty from panicking about the major changes going on in the world."

"The first change that we need to address is ignorance," says Reed. "It's people like..."

Randal cuts him off before he can get another word in. "Okay, that's enough Reed! Now let's go through the presentation."

Sean is sitting at the end of the table and leans over to whisper in Paul's ear.

"You know you need to lay off Reed. He may be the next president of this company."
Paul whispers back. "The board will never elect a freak to run this business. And besides, I hate him. Does that make me a racist or just someone who hates freaks? Look at

him! People only deal with him because they have to. They feel sorry for oppressing people like him for all the bad things we did years ago. We can't change the past, nor should we. He doesn't belong and that's obvious. The fact that we are helping people like him is pathetic and this will be the demise of our company."

Chapter VII

Office Break

Their office was in the newer part of down-
town. There were a lot of tall buildings in the
area. Between the business offices were high-
rise condos where young executives paid exu-
berant prices for small apartments. There
were also parks in the area that helped soften
the feel of the neighborhood given the vast
number of tall buildings and concrete sidewalks. The restaurants that lined the streets
all had tables with umbrellas on the sidewalk
so customers could have lunch or dinner outside. While the day had started off sunny, by
about 10:30am the clouds started rolling in.
Rohan and Sol were programmers and had

decided to take a break from starring at computers all morning. Whenever they took their breaks, they liked to head outside their offices and walk along the sidewalks and engage in "techie" conversation about the newest gadgets or software. Rohan was a seasoned employee at the software company and he knew the ins and outs of the business. He had helped his company grow by more than ten percent each year and had worked his way into a nice corner office. Sol was fresh out of business school but brought many credentials with him. He had won several academic awards in college to go along with his many athletic awards.

Rohan had befriended Sol at work and Sol looked to Rohan as a mentor. Their backgrounds were astonishingly similar. Both came to the business with multiple degrees from Ivy League schools. They both had excelled in sports and graduated college at the top of their class. But there was one principal reason why Rohan went to seek out Sol as soon as Sol joined the company. They both had a beautiful, red skin that was as vibrant as a stop light.

"So you think being smarter than everyone else is what makes you special?" Rohan says smiling at Sol. "Being extraordinarily smart or extremely athletic might separate you from the best of mankind, but that's just scratching the surface. You are much more. You have a special power that only people like us have."

"Power?" Sol says with a perplexed look on his face. "What are you talking about?"

"For years people like us roamed the earth with a power that set us apart from other be-ings," Rohan explains. "We lived in harmony with mankind, not showcasing our power but suppressing it so as to not make other beings feel inferior. Eventually they couldn't deal with our differences and they started to persecute people like us. Hundreds of years went by and people like us forgot how to utilize our powers. We have been successful as a race through being smarter than the masses, but that isn't the only thing that makes us superior to the rest of the world."

Deep down Sol knew that Rohan was speaking the truth.

Rohan continues. "I can't really tell you about it. I have to show you. Let's go for a ride."
"Where are we going?" Sol inquired.
"To the ocean," Rohan says with an even bigger smile.

As they drove to the ocean, it started to rain. Sol didn't know why but for some reason he loved it when it rained. He felt strong and alive, as if he could do anything. He wanted to let the windows down just as they were driving as he would always do in his car, but he wanted to respect Rohan and not get his car's interior wet.

As they approached the ocean, he felt at peace as he usually did when he was close to bodies of water. When he was a young boy he would take long walks along the ocean. It was a time he cherished. It felt as if he got a set of new batteries every time he went and he always came back refreshed.

"Why are we going to the ocean?" Sol asks.

"Because I want to show you something."

"What?" asks Sol.

"Don't worry, you'll know soon enough," Rohan assured him.

When they arrive at the docks, Rohan parks the car and the two men start walking towards the water. The docks extended about two hundred meters towards the ocean, just far enough so that on a foggy day like today, the end of the dock completely disappeared. The raining continued. They didn't have an umbrella, but Sol didn't care. He never used an umbrella. Rohan didn't seem to be bothered by the rain either. They walked to the end of the dock where the fog was thickest. The ocean was particularly active and it felt as if the dock itself was swaying with the waves.

"Can you feel the energy?" Rohan asks.

"Yes," Sol replies.

"Now watch this," says Rohan.

Rohan reaches over the side of the dock and points his hands directly at the water. To Sol's amazement a school of fish of various sizes began to surround the dock; as if Rohan had somehow summoned them. The fish swam near the surface of the water, apparently waiting for his command. Rohan pointed his hands to the right and the fish take off swimming in that direction.

Sol's jaw dropped in amazement, not because of what he had seen, but from the idea of how much power he could potentially have.

Chapter VIII

Inferior Beings

A man named James was pacing around the room. James was in his late 60's. He had beautiful red skin, with no wrinkles, despite his age. Surprisingly, he had the stature of a man in his late twenties or early thirties. He dressed in a younger man's clothing – dark washed jeans, boots and a V-neck t-shirt. He gestured freely with his hands when he spoke and always brought his emotions into his conversations. In his right hand, James always held a bottle of water that he would take a sip almost religiously every hour, on the hour.

James had grown up in a different time. In the 50's and 60's, people of red color started publically separating themselves from the general populous. They were superior in every way, but were oppressed by the masses because there were still very few of them in comparison to other minorities.

"For most of my younger life I was ridiculed," James says in a strong baritone voice. "I was the smartest, most athletic person at my high school, but I was treated like an outcast. I singlehandedly won the state championship for my basketball team four times, yet I got no respect, other than from my teammates. I wanted to fit in, but was never really able to do so. My only girlfriend in high school was ridiculed so much that I broke up with her so she could live the normal life for which I often longed for. Even the teachers treated me differently. I was the smartest person in school, but my teachers saw me as a threat. I stopped asking questions in class because I didn't want them to feel inferior. My papers were heavily scrutinized, unlike the other smart kids. When I was a senior, there was another kid like me. We bonded and I became like a big brother to him. I couldn't stand for people to treat him like they treated me. So I did my best to pave the way for him." James continues. "In college, things were a little better but there were still problems just not as publicly noticeable. I had to start my own business because even though I had graduated head of my class, employers wouldn't hire me. Things are much different now. Our kind is accepted for the most part and if not accepted, tolerated. We have representatives in powerful positions around the world and we are appreciated for our abilities."

"So you have experienced the change in our culture," James says, starring at Nikhil. You have experienced people's understanding of our kind. You have now benefited from your talents. So why do you still harbor anger?"

Nikhil's head was down. He had been deep in thought as he often is. Nikhil was thirty-five years old. He had a manicured beard and mustache. He was wearing a faded t-shirt and old jeans that looked as if he had worn them through many wars. He had a muscular build and often rolled his sleeves up to show off his arms. He, like James, had striking red skin. Like James, he always kept a bottle of water by his side. He looks up and stares at James.

"Because they need to pay for what they put me and my kind through," Nikhil says with passion and anger in his voice. "They need to suffer like we have suffered. They need to be treated like who they really are."

"Inferior beings."

Growing up Nikhil had his share of problems. Just when he thought things couldn't get any worse, Nikhil's father got a new job and his family moved to a new town. The town was even smaller than the one they had lived in and his neighbor's had less tolerance for him and his family. Now Nikhil wasn't worried about kids not talking to him, he was worried about kids trying to beat him up. Every day after the last bell he would run from school to the bus stop and try to get on before any of the other kids. He knew if he hung around, there would be trouble. The other kids learned of his plan and started to chase him to the bus stop every day. They would throw sticks and rocks at him, and shout mean slurs at him.

But no matter how much they chased him, they could never catch him. Nikhil never worried about getting caught. He was so much faster than the other kids. Not only could he outrun the fastest kids in school, he could outrun the rocks that were being thrown at him. But he would always run just fast enough to get away. He didn't want the other kids to think he was more of a freak than they already did.

During recess, teachers would join the students outside, but they really didn't pay much attention to what was going on or the events that transpired each day.

His school playground was unlike most playgrounds. To begin, there was no grass in the school's play areas. There had been grass years ago, but now the play areas were just barren. Underneath the monkey bars and

swings were sheets of concrete. A fence surrounded the playground and the students
would race between the fences, from one side
of the playground to the other, just for fun.
The students would play ball games against
the sides of the school's walls, either baseball
with a spray painted strike zone or a game
called "balls up" where they would throw a
ball against the walls and try to catch it off
the bounce.

Often, a few of the older students would pick
on any kid that had red skin. They would follow that kid around, call him names, taunt
and laugh at him. Nikhil didn't want to get
into it with the other kids, so he was always
running, careful to keep a good distance from
them hoping that they would eventually give
up. Sometimes the older kids would chase
him for the entire period of recess, stopping
only when recess was over.

Once, one of the school's teachers noticed how the other kids were treating Nikhil. When classes resumed, the teacher came into the room and asked Nikhil if he would point out the kids who were harassing him. The students who had been bullying Nikhil started squirming in their seats.

Nikhil slowly looked around the room and said, "No one in this class was harassing me."

The bullies breathed a sigh of relief. Although Nikhil was constantly being picked on, he never tried to retaliate. He did not want to get the other guys in trouble. Yet, even though Nikhil had surely spared the bullies from punishment or even suspension from school, the next day the bullies were at it again. They were relentless – teasing Nikhil, pointing and laughing at him. Nikhil didn't want any trouble but the kids just wouldn't stop. Day after day Nikhil would out run the kids long enough for the bell to ring and he was safely back in the class. He wasn't scared of the kids he just didn't want trouble.

One day Nikhil had had enough. He decided he wasn't going to run anymore. When it was time for recess, like clockwork, the class bullies came over to Nikhil, ready to harass him. This time when they ran toward Nikhil, he didn't move. They were, of course, startled by his action.

As one of the bullies boldly started to walk towards him, Nikhil spoke in a calm voice, "No more – no more of this!"

But the bully wasn't listening to Nikhil. He continued to move aggressively toward Nikhil. The bully tried to shove Nikhil, but Nikhil quickly moved out of the way and tripped him. The bully lost his balance and

tried to break his fall, but he was unsuccess-
ful. He fell forward and landed on his stom-
ach and rolled over on his side. His face and
clothes were covered in dirt and gravel. The
other kids on the playground, who had been
watching this exchange, started laughing
boisterously. As the kids were laughing, the
bully became furious.

The bully stumbled to his feet and started
taking off his jacket. He wanted nothing more
than to clobber Nikhil. Nikhil was now on
guard and felt a surge of adrenaline in a way
he had never felt before. His heart started
beating more rapidly. He broke out in a
sweat. Everything around Nikhil seemed to
slow down. Nikhil could hear that the other
kids on the playground were talking and
laughing, but to Nikhil, it sounded as if they
were slurring their words. Even as the bully
started moving towards him, it seemed to

Nikhil that he was moving in slow motion. The bully's angry advance toward him seemed to take minutes, not seconds. The bully swung his arm to punch him, but Nikhil saw it coming from a mile away. So Nikhil just moved slightly out of the way and the bully went tumbling past him. The bully gathered himself again and turned back toward Nikhil ready to strike with a flurry of punches. Nikhil calmly watched the bully's movement in what seemed to be slow motion, and simply moved away from the clenched fists. By now, the bully was frustrated and even angrier. He kept swinging at Nikhil, but missed every time. Nikhil couldn't believe that the world around him was moving so slowly. The crowd of students couldn't believe the Nikhil was so fast. Nikhil never swung at the bully; he just made sure he was just far enough out of reach so he wouldn't get hit.

The kids continued to laugh at the bully; he looked silly as he continued to swing at Nikhil again and again, in vain. Nikhil was hoping this "fight" would be over quickly and that a teacher would come over and break it up. But there was no teacher in sight. Finally the bully, exhausted and almost defeated, lunged at Nikhil in an attempt to tackle him. Nikhil saw the lunge coming way before it began. Nikhil didn't want to run anymore. He wanted to gain the respect he knew he needed so he wouldn't get picked on again. He decided to stand firm and let the bully try and tackle him. By now the bully was coming at full steam towards Nikhil. It seemed inevitable that Nikhil would have to fight back.

As Nikhil braced for impact, ready to take the blow and hopefully deliver one back, something inexplicable happened. The bully's body made contact with Nikhil, but he bounced of

Nikhil and plopped backwards to the ground with a thud. It was like the bully had run into a wall. The bully was clearly dazed and struggled to get up from the ground with no avail. To the bully, Nikhil's skin felt like stone.

Chapter IX

Assembly

As the men and women entered the room, they were all wearing garments that masked their faces. Most of them wore hats and scarves, while others were wearing hoods, seemingly covering them from the rain. But that wasn't all they were attempting to cover up. This was the first time a group of this size of them had every assembled. For years they had all been drawn to each other but they had never congregated in numbers of more than three. There had been talk of having such a meeting but they all had doubts that it would ever happen. But this was a new year. Unbeknownst to them, this year would change the course of history forever.

This meeting was more than just an opportunity to get people with their unique appearance together. The meeting's purpose was much more urgent than that. For years they had integrated themselves into their communities. They were noticeably different but tried to blend in as much as possible. They had survived several attempted genocides. They had suffered through and survived scientific tests. They had survived public abuse of every kind. But this new foe was much more sinister. They had all started to notice that politicians, scientists and other prominent people like them were starting to disappear, and with no explanation. The local authorities in their perspective cities assembled search teams but to no avail. Government officials weren't offering much help so this group decided it was time to come together to find a solution. Physically, they all had a major thing in common. They all had skin that was a shade of red.

They were also similar mentally. Each one of them was remarkably intelligent. In fact, they were far more mentally advanced than normal human beings. And whenever two or more of them were together, they were able to fully communicate with each other without saying many words.

Raina had made the arrangements for the group to assemble.

"My fellow people, we are gathered here today to address a grave danger for people like us," Raina began, standing in front of the group. "We are starting to see the most promising of our people disappear from the face of the earth. To date, all of our attempts to obtain more information and to get the authorities involved have failed. We are at a point where we need to take things into our own hands if we want to solve this mystery."

She was right. Her people had been showing up missing for over a year, but few of the major media channels ever investigated or wrote about these happenings. It has been rumored that it could be a strategically planned, mass kidnapping but there was no real evidence to prove it. Reports of these disappearances were covered by the news media for a day, maybe two, but then quickly forgotten by reporters and the general public.

Raina continues with conviction in her voice. "We have already lost two senators, four scientists, five professors and countless professional athletes. The only thing in common with these victims is the color of their skin.

They are our people."

"We have been tracking these disappearances and our intelligence teams have come to one disturbing conclusion," Raina continued. "These were not just random disappearances or even kidnappings; they were assassinations. This group has been assembled to solve this mystery and stop this horrifying trend."

As the members listened to the shocking words from Raina, they all knew what needed to be done. They had always known it would eventually come to this but never thought it would be in their lifetimes.

Suddenly, the doors flew open and a man walked into the room. He was a tall and slender man. He wore a hat and was dressed in a perfectly tailored black suit. He moved gracefully to the front of the room and stood directly to the right of Raina.

No one could figure out who the man was, but they all had the feeling that they had met him before.

Once he spoke they all knew exactly who he was. He was more than a legend. The man who was now addressing the assembly was Hezekiah.

"Throughout history, I have individually met with all of our brothers and sisters at some point in their lives. I have provided you with just enough information about our existence so that you would want to seek out the complete story on your own. I have helped you all understand your powers and have encouraged each of you to succeed in all facets of life at levels unfathomable among the general public. We have excelled as a people and have positioned ourselves perfectly as prominent members in society."

Hezekiah pauses and gathers himself before saying. "The only thing left in our way is this new adversary. We must take this enemy head on. We must show no mercy for they have shown no mercy to our brothers and sisters. This enemy has started a chain of events about which our people prophesized many generations ago."

Hezekiah spoke now with an undeniable sense of urgency. "We must crush our enemy and prepare for the next logical transition. The time has come for all of our family to rise up together and take its rightful place in the world. As rulers!"

Chapter X

Story of the Red

Dane was walking home from the bus stop as he had always done. The walk was about ten blocks but it never seemed very long. On this day he saw something he had never seen in this neighborhood. He saw a beggar sitting in the middle of the sidewalk close to the corner of the street. The beggar was blocking the path Dane needed to take to get home. Dane had two options: one would be to change direction and walk across the street; the other would be to pass on the right knowing he would have to get fairly close to the beggar. Dane was not one to shy away from any situation so he chose to pass by close to the beggar. As Dane got closer, he could not see the beggar's face, but he could tell that the beggar was reasonably tall and thin. The beggar's face was covered with a scarf, but Dane could see two eyes peeping out and those eyes were looking him up and down.

Dane was always intrigued by beggars. Sometimes he even doubted they were actually poor. He marveled at their ability to find the best locations to catch the attention of passersby. It seemed that they would always have clever signs; with unique request for food and money. He had heard that in one city, people would beg for money in the streets during the day and in the evening, climb into their cars and drive home to their mansions.

As he got even closer to the beggar, Dane tried to make out what was on the beggar's cardboard sign. The sign read, "Any money you can donate would be much appreciated and in return I will provide you with knowledge that is priceless."

This was by far the most interesting request for money that he had ever seen. He felt compelled to stop and speak to the beggar to see what kind of knowledge the beggar might impart to him. By now, Dane was almost standing in front of the beggar. As he approached the beggar, he reached into his pocket and pulled out a little over a dollar in change.

Smirking a bit, Dane asked, "What kind of knowledge could you possibly give me?"

Dane found that he was always the smartest person in the room. He prided himself with having more knowledge under his finger than most had in their entire body. He had thought all of his life that he was just smarter than the average person, but nothing more than that.

The beggar looked up and at that instance, Dane could see that the beggar was in fact a woman. Despite the fact that she was wearing a large hat that covered most of her face, Dane could see that she had the blackest pupils he had ever seen which gave her a sinister appearance. Her presence was dark and mysterious, yet familiar.

The woman held out her hand to take the money that Dane offered and in the most beautiful and calming voice that Dane had ever heard.

The woman then said, "Thank you, Dane. My name is Alethea. How much time do you have?"

Interesting question, Dane thought.

"As much time as needed to get my knowledge worth," Dane replied.

Alethea looked deep into Dane's eyes and said, "The knowledge I am about to give you has no price tag to it; it is priceless."

Dane was intrigued. "Please continue," he said.

Alethea continued, "What I am about to tell you will open your eyes and provide insight into your existence in this world and what your destiny entails. You will look at yourself and everyone around you in a different light. There are things in life we have control over and things that are out of our control. For instance, your destiny. We run from it most of our lives, but eventually we have to face it and embrace its direction."

She went on. "The only thing I ask is for your full attention because there will be a time when you will have to retell this story to one of our people and provide him or her with enlightenment."

Alethea made herself comfortable on a bench close to the corner of the street and Dane sat down next to her. Then Alethea looked him in the eyes and said, "Have you ever heard of the 'Story of the Red'?"

Chapter XI

The Beginning

Alethea begins to tell her story.

In the beginning, many years ago there existed an island nation, located in the middle of the Atlantic Ocean and populated by a noble and powerful race. The people of this land possessed great wealth because of the natural resources that could be found throughout their island. The island was a center for trade and commerce. The rulers of this land held sway over the people of the island as well as many other parts of the world.

This island was the domain of a powerful being named Kabir who was the "god of the sea." Kabir had a beautiful red skin that could absorb and reflect light as well. He fell in love with a mortal woman, Anya, and created a dwelling for the two of them at the top of a hill near the middle of the island. He surrounded the dwelling with rings of water and land to protect her.

Anya gave birth to five sets of twin boys who became the first rulers of this land. As the boys came of age, Kabir divided the island among the brothers. The eldest, Dilip, was in line to be the island's first King. Kabir gave him control over the central hill and all surrounding areas.

At the top of the central hill, the people of the island built a temple to honor Kabir. The temple housed a giant gold statue of Kabir riding a chariot pulled by winged horses. It was here that the rulers of this land would come to discuss laws, pass judgments, and pay tribute to Kabir.

To facilitate travel and trade, the civilians dug a water canal that cut through the ring of water that enabled water to also run south straight to the ocean.

The main city of the island was named Dominar, meaning "great city," and it was located just outside the outer ring of water covering a stretch of many miles. This was a densely populated area. The climate was very humid such that two harvests were possible each year, one in the winter that was fed by the rains and one in the summer that was fed by irrigation from the canal. Surrounding the plain to the north were mountains that soared to the skies. Villages, lakes, rivers, and meadows dotted the mountains.

Besides the harvests, the island provided all

kinds of herbs, fruits, and nuts and an abundance of animals, including elephants, roamed the island.

For generations, the people lived simple, virtuous lives. But slowly they began to change. Greed and power began to corrupt them. They say the next events were an act of God determining a suitable punishment for their corruption. They say the ocean opened up and swallowed the island, its people and its memory.

People have been searching for the location and remains of this island for years. It is said that because the people of that island were so powerful and resourceful they rebuilt their city and continued to thrive...underwater.

Chapter XII

Giant

"The next account of red in history is as follows," said Alethea.

By the age of seventeen he had grown to four cubits and a span tall (six feet, nine inches). He was of muscular build with the strength of ten men. He only wore a cloth tied around his waist and boots. His muscles rippled beneath a red skin that was like solid steel to the touch.

He was a fierce warrior and his size made him practically invincible. Because of his menacing stature he would strike fear in all of

his opponents, often winning the battle before any clash of spears.

His army proudly displaced this warrior as a
symbol of their dominance. Sometimes the
men of the army would bring out this fierce
warrior late in the battle, when victory was
almost at hand to further crush any hopes
their opponents had of winning. At other
times, the leaders of the army would show
their warrior before the battle for all the opponents to see, to instill doubt that they
would have any chance to survive the battle.

He would often kill men with his bare hands
and had never lost in hand-to-hand combat.
Other armies would send their best warrior to
fight him, all with the same outcome, defeat.

As his army was invading a new foe, they
called out to have the opponent's army send

out their best warriors to fight in a one-on-one, hand-to-hand combat with their champion. Only one man was brave enough to fight this warrior. This brave man was not a soldier, but he had the courage of a general. He did not wear any armor and had an unconventional selection for a weapon.

The field upon which these two warriors would be engaged in conflict was stained with the blood of men from previous battles. It was an open field. There were no places to hide or run from the enemy. On this day of battle, it was hot and humid. It was early afternoon so the sun was bright and created a glaring shadow that could distract the two fighters. The two armies were aligned around the open field in a circle, not engaging in physical battle, but hurling verbal insults at each other. The ground was firm so there was no chance of slipping while making moves to attack your opponent. The area set up well for the giant. There was plenty of space for him to maneuver his large weapons and utilize his size to his advantage.

For the giant the open field was like a stage. The attention of both armies was focused on him and he liked it this way. The giant was ready to do what he did best, engage in combat. He felt confident in battle situations. He never doubted his ability to fight or that he would not be the victor.

As the two warriors met in the field of battle, the giant flaunted his size and strength by flexing his muscles and pounding his chest. The giant postured around, mocking the smaller man which generated great laughter amongst his fellow soldiers.

The smaller man was not fazed by all of the

pomposity. He just waited for his opportunity to strike. The giant charged at the smaller man with the speed of a rhino. The smaller man reared back and launched his weapon from his hands. The weapon struck the giant with a fatal blow to the center of his head and down goes the giant.

Chapter XIII

East

Alethea sits up and leans back on the bench, as if she is making sure her posture is perfect and continues her story.

Son was running through the woods as he had always done, flying though the trees, leaping over logs and running so fast over the streams that it looked as if he was running on water. This was the time he loved. He felt free. He couldn't show his powers in his village because his parents didn't want other people to think he was a freak. He had a beautiful red skin and it turned to a dark maroon in the sun. He was smarter and stronger than all of the other people in the village, even the adults. There was nothing left for him to learn in his village and because of this, he longed to go to a city where there might be more people like him. His parents said he was special; that he was a gift from the gods. The other boys and girls in his village often ridiculed him and teased him because of his skin color. But they would all marvel at him if they only knew the power he had. Son was as fast as a cheetah and as strong as an elephant. He could swim for days and could hold his breath under water for seemingly hours. He glided through the trees like an ape and jumped with the spring of a frog. No one knew this in his town. His parents lectured him constantly about never letting anyone know of his powers.

So he would take refuge in the woods where no one was around except the animals. He knew that the animals couldn't tell his secret.

As he was running, he came across a stretch of land that he loved. There was a patch of trees along a river. The river had a steady current and only the strongest swimmers would ever attempt to swim in this river. Years ago, the villagers staged a contest to see if any men in the village could swim across the river. No one was ever able to swim across the river because of the undercurrent. The only way to get across the river was by boat or the roped bridge that had been crafted by the village ancestors.

Son's routine was to swing through the trees next to the river and then dive into the water and swim across to the other side. He felt more comfortable in the water than on land. He felt a kind of serenity as the water rushed around him and he was even more comfortable when he was totally submerged beneath the surface of the water.

Some days Son would just dive in and start swimming at a blistering pace. Any other person would have had trouble swimming, but he seemed to glide against the tremendous current. Other swimmers would have to use both arms and legs to make any progress in the water. Son was such a great swimmer that he could navigate through the current by just kicking his legs. Sometimes he would swim under water the entire width of the river. He would often catch and bring back bags of exotic fish that he would sell for a great price in the village.

This day Son gathered a large bag of the best fish and began the journey home. He was about 30 miles away from the village, but since he was so fast, he could usually cover the distance in about 30 minutes. He never ever told anyone in the village where he found the fish. They wouldn't believe him. No one ever caught fish from this river and the expedition to get there would take most of the day. So he just told the villagers that he went fishing and got lucky.

This particular journey back to the village was different. He felt uneasy about the trip. The animals seemed agitated and restless. He couldn't put his finger on it but there was definitely a feeling of tension all around him. As he sped through the woods, he noticed a herd of gazelles running frantically in one direction. They seemed as if they were running for their lives.

Then he saw what the cause of all of the commotion was. A lion, as tall as a man, was feasting on a gazelle. He had never seen a lion so large. Son slowed down to get a better look. The lion's head was the size of an elephant's head and his paws were as big as the feet of a hippopotamus. The lion was truly a menacing sight, but also a truly beautiful creature. As Son moved closer, he felt as if he was being watched or maybe even hunted.

Suddenly, another lion jumped out from the bushes behind him. This lion was just as big and its movements were as quick as lightning. He barely dogged the swipe of the lion's paw and started to run as fast as he could. Both lions got a whiff of the fish that Son was carrying and they were in pursuit of him to get the fish and possibly Son, too. Son normally felt comfortable being around animals, but these lions were different. They had a special coloring that was as unique as their size. Instead of a light brown coloring, these lions had a fur that looked as if it was an amber shade of red.

The lions were gaining on Son and he knew the time would come when he would have to stop running and eventually face the lions in battle. If he could just hold on for a little longer, he knew that the lions would eventually give up pursuit.

Son knew he had a great chance to outrun the lions because when he was younger and not as fast, he outran a cheetah the fastest animal on land. He focused on the path in front of him. He had run this way many times. He knew this path like the back of his hand. He knew where to cut right or jump. He knew where he could swing on a tree or run through a pond. He knew that eventually he would lose the lions.

But something happened that had never happened before. The lions were gaining on him. They were running past packs of gazelles and other animals that were normally their natural prey. The lions were not distracted by what would have been an easy kill. It seemed like the lions were in pursuit of Son just for the challenge, a challenge for which they had been longing, a challenge that rivaled their superior fighting skills. One lion broke off from the chase and took a different route. Son wondered why, but he knew he had to focus if he was going to get away from the lion still directly behind him in pursuit.

He was running as fast as he had ever run and he started to run even faster. He had never pushed himself to this level so he was tapping into something he had never thought possible. He knew there was definitely a limit to his abilities and thought he had previously reached it. With his heightened level of focus and the eminent danger, he pushed himself harder than ever before.

Then something impossible happened. The other lion was coming at him from his side at an angle to intercept him. But how could this lion have outrun him? How could the lion have run so fast that he had ultimately passed him? Upon this realization, Son slowed down and stopped running. He stood up tall, gathered himself and grabbed the small knife that was tucked inside his belt.

Son knew it was finally time. Time to fight!

Chapter XIV

Kingdom

Alethea continued...another person linked to your ancestry was born in 69BC. She was born into a dynastic family that governed a vast empire. She had been in power since the time of her youth, starting out ruling jointly with her father and later with her two brothers.

The area she ruled was a strip of land along a great river. Every year the river would flood its banks, and then recede leaving rich fertile soil for growing crops. The land surrounding her empire was a barren desert which stretched as far as the eye could see. This land served as protection against potential invaders.

Eventually she became the sole ruler of the empire. Her skin had an auburn tone that glistened in the sunlight and glowed under moonlit skies. People initially thought she inherited her coloring due to a high degree of inbreeding in her family. She was described by her people as a woman of surpassing beauty. She also possessed a most charming voice and knowledge of how to influence anyone. Being so beautiful to look upon and to listen to, with the power to subjugate everyone, she masterfully used it to her advantage.

Her parents were brother and sister and because of that she had only one set of grandparents. Those grandparents were uncle and niece, again limiting the number of ancestors and diversity in the bloodlines. She was not a native of the land she had governed so she studied their culture, learned the language and positioned herself as the reincarnation of one of her people's most illustrious gods. She continued to stay in power by making strategic alliances with the most powerful men of her time, along with making sure she promoted her children into ruling positions.

Her empire included land that had a plentiful source of precious metals and semi-precious stones. This made her kingdom one of the world's most powerful and wealthiest civilizations. Unlike other royalty of her time, she did not rule by fear. All of the members of her kingdom adored her and would go blindly into war if she commanded it. It was said that her unique ability to convince people to do her will and grant her whishes, was magical. It was almost like she could hypnotize a person with just the sound of her voice.

Chapter XV

Leader

Alethea looks into Dane's eyes and continues with another story. Amazingly, Mulai was the leader of his tribe at age fifteen. He was the strongest and the wisest of his people. He had shown his leadership in many ways and was braver than men three times his age. His legend started at an early age with feats of strategy and strength, unmatched by any man.

When Mulai was ten, he had an encounter with three tigers that, driven by hunger, had surmounted an attack on his immediate family. One evening his family was out for a walk near the woods to gather food to eat as they would always do together at least once a day. At the first sight of the tigers, Mulai knew he had to protect his mother and younger siblings; who would not survive an attack by such fierce creatures. He looked around the area for something he could use for a weapon, but there was nothing in sight. He would have to engage the tigers with his bare hands. He ordered his family to run and climb a nearby tree to safety while he held off the tigers. Tigers instinctively have a certain way to attack their prey. They silently creep up on their prey when their prey tries to escape; they chase them down, striking with swift blows with their claws. Once their prey had fallen, they used their sharp teeth to pierce the skin and kill the victim.

The first tiger walked towards the family, ready to pounce, but hesitated. Mulai wasn't moving. There would be no chase in this attack. Mulai knew he had to stand his ground. The alternative running away from the tiger would mean an inevitable slaughter. The tiger attackcd with a blinding speed and took a swipe at Mulai. But Mulai blocked his claw with his left hand and grabbed the neck of the tiger with his right hand. He then threw the tiger back twenty feet into the nearby bushes. By this time, the second tiger had taken a swipe at him, but Mulai was ready. Mulai moved with a quickness that rivaled the tiger's speed and got behind the tiger grabbing its head in the process. With a quick twist, Mulai broke the tiger's neck, killing it instantly. The third tiger had moved in while Mulai was still wrestling with the second tiger. The third tiger leapt on top of Mulai and took a bite at his leg. This bite surely would have crushed every bone in Mulai's leg but the tiger's sharp teeth didn't even pierce Mulai's skin. Mulai grabbed the sides of the ti-

ger's mouth and pulled at the corners, shat-
tering its jaw in the process. Mulai then cast
the tiger aside and readied himself for the
next attack. As he turned around to get his
bearings, the first tiger was back up, but it
didn't attack him. Mulai stared into the eyes
of the tiger and the tiger retreated back into
the woods.

Mulai grew into a skilled warrior. He special-
ized in guerilla warfare and led numerous
war parties against armies and towns. His hit
-and run strategies were legendary and with
his successes, he rose to be supreme chief of
his tribe.

Mulai would go on to lead his tribe into battle
against many enemies. Most of the time Mulai and his tribe would fight alone, protecting
each other from vicious enemy attacks. Other
times Mulai would partner with neighboring

tribes and lead them all to victory.

Mulai would then conduct special ceremonies with the neighboring tribes after their successful war collaborations. During one of the ceremonies, he had a premonition that his people would be victorious in a huge battle where his fiercest opposition would be destroyed.

Not long after the ceremony, his tribe was invaded by an enemy like no other. This army was skilled in all types of combat and, as a result, caught Mulai's tribe by surprise. While this opponent was a formidable one, the army had made one huge mistake. They had vastly underestimated the size and will of Mulai's tribe. The opposing army was eventually defeated in a great battle, fulfilling the predicted outcome and cementing Mulai's legendary status.

There was an old prophecy that went back to the beginning of his people that there would be a person who would eventually bring Mulai's people to prominence. By the time Mulai was thirty, he had already helped his tribe become completely self-sufficient. For many years, Mulai's tribe was reliant on neighboring tribes for food, water and safe shelter.

Mulai had devised a plan that would end the need for any trade or help from others. His tribe was able to build a small village and feed and shelter all of its inhabitants. They all grew stronger because they had proper nutrition and practiced a form of training to enhance their health. The tribe was never ravished by disease because Mulai had developed natural remedies for all of their sickness. In a few years they had become strong enough to stand up to all of the other enemy tribes that wanted to take resources from them. He consulted with the leaders of the other tribes and sold them products that were sought after at a high price.

These products made Mulai's tribe rich and even more powerful. But with this new power, they started to have a different problem. More outside tribes wanted to take what they had. It soon became inevitable that they would have to develop a new plan to better defend themselves. Mulai took the strongest men in the tribe and built a natural perimeter made of dirt and gravel around the area of his village. He instructed tribesmen to build a mote outside of the perimeter and fill it with water. Anyone who wanted to attack would have to cross fifty yards of water first before they reached the perimeter. In addition, Mulai instructed his people to build a ninety foot wall made of stone behind the perimeter that would deflect all forms of attack including arrows, spears, large stones and even fire.

He had trained his people in combat and more importantly, he taught them how they could be strong together.

Mulai continued to rule his tribe for many years. He was said to have magical healing powers and that he could command elements from both the physical world and the spiritual world to cure any ailments. People would travel vast distances, across miles of land, sea and mountains to be treated by Mulai.

By the time Mulai had passed the leadership of his tribe to his first son, his tribe had grown in size to tens of thousands.

"Shall I continue or have you heard enough," said Alethea seemingly already knowing the answer.

Dane was so engulfed in Alethea's stories that he had to hear more. It was as if his eyes had been shut all of his life and were finally opening.

"No, please tell me more," Dane replied.

Chapter XVI

Unification

Alethea takes a pause from her story telling to have another drink of water. She clears her throat and jumps right into her next story. One would have never guessed from the outside looking in that this group of volcanic and coral islands in the central Pacific Ocean was the habitat of such fascinating countryside. The land was filled with a surplus of tropical forests and exotic fruits after which people from many lands sought. There were eight major islands and more than one hundred minor ones. The islands were first discovered around 700 A.D., by humans who were voyaging across thousands of miles of ocean in mat-sailed, double canoes. By the end of the 16th century, having lived isolated from the rest of the world for close to 1000 years, they had divided their eight islands into four occasionally warring chiefdoms.

Around the mid 1700's, a warrior was born who would one day fulfill a great prophecy. The prophecy was foretold of a male child who would rise to power and become a mighty conqueror of many chiefdoms. This warrior would become the king of this land and eventually unify all of the neighboring lands around him. Because of this prophecy, current leaders did everything in their power to identify this child and eliminate him.

Once the future warrior was born, his family knew of the prophecy and what the leaders had planned to do. So they sent him to live with his relatives in the mountains. There the child existed in virtual solitude as a youth. His name was Kenan. As a young man, he was taught by his oldest relative the skills he would need to become a great leader. He studied the ancient chants that provided instructions on how speak to and relate to the gods. He was skilled in vigorous water and land sports that ultimately would assist him in the field of battle. He also excelled in games of the mind and had an ability to strategize war formations that rivaled even the elders.

He exhibited feats of strength that no one could explain and no other man could accomplish. He once moved a stone that weighed well over two tons with his bare hands. There was a legend among his people that whoever could move this particular stone would one day unite all of the islands.

During one of Kenan's training sessions, he instructed his sparring partners to hurl six spears at him, all at the same time. Kenan caught three in one hand as they flew at him. He broke two by hitting them with another spear he carried in his other hand and the last one he dodged.

By the time Kenan was a full grown man he had a tall, slender physique and was extremely agile and fearless. He was skilled in all forms of combat. He was strong-willed and could think clearly and effectively in any situation. He had an uncanny way of inspiring loyalty amongst his followers.

Kenan eventually became the leader of his army, led countless raids on the neighboring islands and was part of many battles before taking his rightful place as King.

For the rest of his life he ruled in peace, building a powerful government and establishing a profitable trade and agricultural industry for his land.

There is mention in the history books that his skin had the color of a red hard-shelled crab.

Chapter XVII

War

As she leans against the back of the bench using her shoulder to support herself, Alethea continues.

In the early 1900's, World War I was won in the trenches. There were many heroic stories of war in the history books, but there was one untold story.

With the moon blocked by dense clouds, the night was exceptionally dark. The tall trees and heavy brush made it almost impossible to determine direction. Rain was coming down in buckets, which only enhanced the navigational challenges. Visibility was less than ten feet. In the background you could hear bombs going off and bullets flying, but there were no indications of the direction from which the enemy was coming. The army had run out of food and water having been in the field, away from base for a couple of weeks. The small, special operations group started out with fifty men and had slowly dwindled down to about twenty-five through the course of battle. This loss might have killed the moral of most troops, but not these men.

It had been raining for three days but the tide was turning in the war. Two soldiers had stood out in the field of battle. Their tireless, relentless pursuit of the enemy went beyond some aspects of human capability. They both had fought through countless injuries that would have crippled average men.

The rest of the team thought these two soldiers were brothers. They both were of similar height and had a slender build. Their skin
had a deep cherry tint that glowed even in the
darkness and heavy rain.

The two soldiers seemed to thrive in the rain
and moved though the adverse environment
as if they were somehow controlling the elements. They seemed to be able to anticipate
the enemy's movement and had an uncanny
ability to see things in the darkness, seeing
things others couldn't. For these two men,
the rain gave them an advantage and they
knew they had to make the most of this opportunity if they wanted to get their fellow
soldiers back to the base.

As the team of twenty-five men worked their
way through the brush, all of a sudden it was
surprisingly quiet. The soldiers could hear

neither bullets whizzing by nor bombs exploding. This could mean one of two things, either the enemy had retreated or they were walking into a trap!

The soldiers assumed the latter, so they slowed their cadence and tried to analyze what possible situations they might be walking into. The two soldiers; whose names were Jacob and David, took the lead and went out to scout the environment.

"What do you think?" Jacob asked David.
"I think we should first check the perimeter to get a better idea of what we are up against," replied David.
"Okay," said Jacob. "Let me get up higher for a better view."

Jacob started scaling a nearby tree. He scaled the tree with the agility of a squirrel even

though he did not have any climbing equip-
ment. Leaping from limb to limb, he continued to ascend to the top of the tree where he
could get a better view. Close to the top was a
perch where he sat to adequately assess the
situation. What he saw was astonishing. A
little more than a hundred yards ahead of the
team was a massive army. The army was
moving quickly into position to attack the un-
suspecting team.

Jacob descended from the tree at the speed of
a free fall and made it to the bottom almost
instantly. "We have to go now!" Jacob said
with a sudden urgency.

"What did you see?" David asked.

"It's an ambush. We have to tell the team to
retreat to the north."

Jacob and David ran back to alert the troops
of their findings. Heeding the warning, the

team of soldiers took off in several directions, away from the approaching army. With the oncoming enemy army closing in quickly the troops knew they would have to weigh their options and make some quick decisions. They decided that if they had any chance for the group to get away safely they would need volunteers to stay back to provide cover. Of course Jacob and David volunteered. It made the most sense because everyone knew that if any of the troops successfully could divert the enemy soldiers, it would be them.

David asked Jacob, "What's your plan?"

"We just have to give the team enough of a head start so they won't be caught."

"So, what's your plan?" David asked again with a confused look on his face.

"Let's get to higher ground and wage a counterattack. This should catch them off guard and buy the team some time."

"Then what?"

"We make our escape."

"How?"

"Working on that," said David. "Come on, let's climb."

The two men started climbing adjacent trees looking for the perfect perch where they could launch an attack. They both nestled into spaces where they wouldn't be seen from the ground but where they would have a clear vision of what was going on below. They had been in impossible situations in the past but this was definitely the most daunting. The rain started coming down even harder and they knew it would be the cover they needed to surprise the enemy soldiers.

One by one, the enemy soldiers began to fall. Because of the heavy rain, the enemy soldiers couldn't see what was going on. They could only hear their fellow soldiers crying out for help. Then there was silence. A frenzied chaos ensued. Not knowing the location of their attackers, the enemy soldiers started shooting in all directions hoping to strike the attackers.

In less than an hour, David and Jacob had destroyed the army, their numbers dwindling down to four men. In an effort to see from which direction their attackers were coming, the four remaining enemy soldiers stood back to back.

Then, one of the men fell to the ground, a knife stuck in his side. The remaining three men panicked. One of them started screaming loudly and running away from the group as fast as he could. The next sound the remaining two soldiers heard was their fellow fighter crying out for help. Then silence. Suddenly a whistling sound broke the silence as if something was flying towards the two fighters at an incredible pace. Then, one of the two men fell to the ground. A small spear was lodged in his chest.

The last man fell to his knees and screamed, "I surrender, please don't kill me!"

He turned to his right and saw two men moving towards him at speeds no normal human could achieve. As they got closer, all he saw was a red blur. He then realized that the red he was seeing was his own blood.

Chapter XVIII

Future of Red

"Some of these events may have sounded familiar to you," said Alethea. "You may have read these stories as a child or learned about them in school. For the most part the stories are true, but there is a layer that you won't find in history books. History has been altered to protect the innocent and the guilty."

"The one thing to keep in mind is that there is a thin line between the past and the future," Alethea continues. "It's all connected. Every event, even if it's of little significance, can trigger an action that could have major effects on our existence and change the world as we know it. Knowing the true past will help you predict the future. This understanding has been difficult to foresee because certain aspects of our past had been tampered with, and manipulated by others. Making the future far more challenging for people to anticipate. Because I know the true past, the future has become an open book for me to read."

Dane was even more intrigued. Who was this person who was on the street and how did she claim to know everything?

For the first time in his life, things were starting to make sense. He had always had questions about his existence and people like him, but he never had any clear answers that made any sense. He had heard stories about science experiments, mutations, even curses.

Dane felt compelled to get more information. He asked, "If you have a clear vision of the future, what's next? What will happen to people like me? Do we have an integral part to play in the future of the world or will we fade away into obscurity?"

Alethea seemed to have been waiting for these questions. With a huge smile, she stared into Dane's eyes as if she could read his mind. She leaned back on the bench to get more comfortable. She took a large chug of water from her water bottle and then took a deep breath. As she breathed out and cleared her voice, Alethea started to speak.

"The future of Red is more intriguing than the past."

Chapter XIX

With Great Power

"Why are we sympathetic to them when all they have done is treated us like outcasts?" Nikhil said.

"We have been successful in every aspect in life," responds Tomlin. We have doctors, lawyers, scientist, and politicians. We even have the vice president of the United States as one of us."

Although Tomlin had been persecuted most of his life, he always had a good perspective on his abilities and purpose.

Tomlin always knew he was special. Back

when he was in high school, he had managed to get all A's without ever taking a book home or studying for a test. The classes all made sense to him. It was almost as if he had taken them before. Even though getting good grades was extremely easy for him, it was not his passion. His passion was sports and he ultimately excelled in every activity he tried. Despite his slight build, he was a four-year starting quarterback on the Varsity football team. He had surpassed the career high school passing record at the start of his junior year. He was a four-year starter on the Varsity basketball team and led the state in scoring and steals. He could have led the nation in any statistic he wanted, if he was interested. He had been a great swimmer his entire life and joined the swim team in high school. Throughout his high school career he had never lost an individual race. He was a three-year starter in baseball and was drafted to play in the minor league during his junior year. He didn't go because he never really wanted to play baseball; he was just good at it.

In addition to his accomplishments, Tomlin looked different from other kids. He had a beautiful red skin that turned auburn in the summer.

When parents and spectators watched Tomlin when he was playing football or basketball or baseball, they would try to analyze him and made comments suggesting that his skin color must be giving him an unfair advantage over the other players. Some parents would say, "That Tomlin kid has some kind of genetic advantage over everyone else." Or they would say, "It's not fair the advantage he has. He should be banned from high school sports." Or even meaner things like, "Look at his skin, he is an abomination."

The parents would also call him names and taunt behind his back and to his face. It happened so much that Tomlin began to get used to it. He would just use the negative comments as fuel to do better and stay motivated.

He was also use to being hazed. From the time he was in grade school, he had had to deal with it. Before grade school kids didn't judge you by the color of your skin. They just wanted to be your friend because you were you. They didn't have the prejudices that adults have. They didn't notice differences in people. Everyone was the same. But in grade school, things started to change. The boys and girls started to get mean. They started ignoring Tomlin, then teasing and chasing him, then hitting Tomlin for no apparent reason other than because he was different. The kids started to band together with other kids. Because Tomlin was different and there was no one else in the school like him, he was considered an outcast. The kids didn't let Tomlin play with them. They wouldn't talk to him. They wouldn't even sit with him at lunch. How could someone feel so lonely amongst so many people?

Tomlin remembers having a conversation with his father when he was thirteen years old. He remembers sitting in the kitchen. Their house was on the large side, seven thousand square feet in size with more room than the family of three could ever need. It was late in the afternoon, but at this time of year the sun didn't set until about 9:00 pm in the evening. His father had just dimmed the lights in the kitchen because the sun was bright and shining through the window.

"Daddy, the kids at school call me names,"

said Tomlin"

"Like what son?"

"They call me a red-faced stepchild. They say I was adopted because I don't look like you or Mommy. They say you two aren't my real parents because my real parents didn't want me."

Tomlin's father was clearly appalled upon hearing this news but he tried to mask his anger in front of Tomlin.

Tomlin's father said, "That is pretty harsh. Are these friends of yours?"

"Not yet, but they are the cool kids in school so I want to be their friends."

"Do you think that if you are their friends that would make you cool?"

"Yes."

"So tell me, what the benefits of being friends with them?"

"Well, they are the older kids so they know everybody. All the younger kids look up to them. The older kids know all of the cool things to say and to do. They are the kids that know where all the cool parties are. They are accepted and they blend into the crowd so much that they can do things and not be noticed."

"What else?" His father asked.

Tomlin responds, "all of the other kids think they are cool. The older kids have cool clothes and the even have their own mopeds"

"Well you are too young to ride a moped so you won't be getting one anytime soon," his father said with a stern but loving voice. "And is there something wrong with your clothes?"

"Yes...I don't dress like the other kids at school. I still dress like the kids in the city so I don't fit in at this school."

"Well son, we can buy you more clothes, but do you really want that. You have good clothes which are a lot better than the ones I had when I was a kid."

Tomlin answers, "I know and I am thankful for what I have. But I just don't fit in."

"Is it the clothes or something else?" his father asked with an inquisitive look.

"Well, I think it's mostly because of my skin. The other kids say I'm an alien or a freak. There are only a couple of kids that have red skin and they are picked on in the same way."

His father responded, "Well I know that this is an important time in your life and it's important to fit in, but that is something that will probably not happen. We talked about this. We told you that when we moved to a smaller city in the northwest there might be the possibility that the other kids wouldn't understand that you are special."

"If I was special then they wouldn't pick on me." Tomlin's voice cracked a bit. "How could I be special and the other kids not recognize it?" His tone became angry and sad at the same time. "I'm not special. I'm just an outcast to them."

"That's not true son," his father tried to reassure him. "You are a unique young man and what makes you special also separates you from the other kids."

"But I don't want to be special."

Hearing the sadness in his son's voice and seeing the sadness in his eyes, Tomlin's father paused and tried to soften his tone and his words.

"Remember all the times I told you that being special carries with it a unique responsibility?" "Answer me this," his father said with a slight smile. "You are a freshman in high school and how did you do in football?"

"What do you mean? Tomlin asks."

"How did you perform this year for the team?"

"I played well," Tomlin responded with a gleam in his eye.

"You played more than just well; you started on the varsity football team as a freshman. And you did what no other freshman has ever done. You started as the quarterback of the team. Do your other football teammates think you're weird?"

"No."

"How did you do in basketball this year?"

"I started."

Tomlin is now sitting straight up and has a glow of confidence.

"Do your basketball teammates think you are weird?" Tomlin's father asked.

"No."

Tomlin's father goes on, knowing he is on a roll. "You are taking AP classes in every subject. Do your classmates think you are weird?"

"Kind of," Tomlin responded with a sheepish grin."

"Well," his father chuckles, "I've seen some of your classmates and they are ones to talk."

(they both laugh)

Tomlin's father goes on. "You are special and everyone sees that. A lot of times when people are envious they tend to try and bring other people down to their level. It makes them feel better about themselves. You have a gift that none of the other kids have. You are a powerful young man in every way."

Then his father said something that he would always remember.

"With great power comes great responsibility!"

As Tomlin and Nikhil continued their conversation, Nikhil is noticeably frustrated with Tomlin's perspective on how they had been treated in their lives.

Nikhil starts speaking with an angry tone. "We don't have prominent people in society because the majority has an affinity for us. The only reason we have anything is because we are smarter, stronger, we work harder and are superior." Nikhil continues. "In twenty years our numbers will grow and we will represent twenty percent of the population. That's enough to totally…"

"Totally what? Tomlin asks."

"Totally take over the world."

"What do you mean?" Tomlin pleads. "Shall the rest of the world be subservient to us? Are you suggesting that we basically enslave them?"

"Only if they resist our rule," Nikhil responds.

"We are the dominant species, we should be treated accordingly."

"You sound like someone who has been consumed by the illusion of absolute power, Tomlin said. "You know what they say -- with great power comes great responsibility and with ultimate power comes ultimate corruption."

"What is corrupt?" Nikhil asks with a disturbing smile. "Has any successful person in this world not been corrupt? I think the definition should be changed to mirror ambition. Am I corrupt or just ambitious?"

"You are ambitious with narrow thoughts that are centered around corruption." Tomlin responds then laughs out loud.

"You will see things my way soon enough," Nikhil fires back. "Have you ever wanted to get the people back that teased you as a child, for making you an outcast as if you had some rare disease?"

Tomlin responds quickly, "Yes, I had a lot of hatred in my youth and I did eventually get them back. I forced my will on the oppressors and the system to become financially wealthy, powerful and respected by friends and foes."

"Is that all you want?" Nikhil stared into Tomlin's eyes. "Is that enough for you? Because it's not for me; I want more."

Chapter XX

The Bridge

Oliver was driving home as he always had done. He liked the drive for a lot of reasons. Firstly, it was his only chance to have some *alone* time when he could think clearly. He also liked this drive because he had just purchased his dream car; a sports sedan with all of the possible upgrades. Driving to work and back home each day was truly a joy. This night was different. It was still light outside but he could see a full moon rising in the east. It lookcd likc it might rain from the patch of dark clouds he saw in the west. The air was cool and humid. He could tell autumn was right around the corner. It had been an unusually dry summer and any rain at this point would be welcome. Whether it rained or not didn't concern him at the time. All that mattered was he was driving home and enjoying one of his most special times of the day. This next portion of the drive Oliver especially enjoyed. He was driving onto a steel bridge over the largest lake in the area. He always marveled in the architecture of the bridge and loved the sound of the steel base underneath his car.

Oliver looked in his rear view mirror and saw an SUV driving up behind him at a fast speed. He changed lanes and sped up a bit. The SUV also changed lanes and continued to follow him. Oliver quickly tried to change lanes again, but by then it was too late. The SUV had rammed his car from behind completely destroying his back fender and trunk. But there was something different about this accident. It really didn't feel like an accident.

Oliver pulled over to the side of the bridge and turned the car off. He took his seatbelt off with the intent of getting out of the car to talk to the other driver when he felt another jolt from behind and a loud crashing sound. The driver had hit Oliver's car again and was pushing it with his SUV. Oliver held on to the steering wheel and thought about calling the police but didn't want to take his hands off the steering wheel.

At that point Oliver took a survey of his surroundings. He started to panic because he was on a bridge and his car was getting dangerously close to the edge. His foot was on the break but the SUV behind him was more powerful and continued to push his car. It was inevitable that he was going to hit the edge of the bridge. There was a barrier but it didn't look strong enough to stop his car from

going over the side of bridge. Then it happened. His car was teetering over the side.
Oliver's mind was racing. He knew there
would be two things for which he would need
to prepare, one would be the impact of his car
hitting the water and the second would be
that the water would eventually flood his car.
Suddenly his panic subsided and he became
unusually calm. His car started to fall over
the side of the bridge. It seemed as if the car
was falling for minutes even though he knew
it was only seconds that were passing. Oliver
had just enough time to brace for the impact
and contemplate his next move. His car hit
the water with a thunderous thud. After that
it immediately started to sink.

When the car was completely submerged in
the water, Oliver decided it was time to break
the window and try to get out. Water was
rushing in the car through a crack in the win-

dow faster than he expected.   He knew it would only be seconds before the inside was completely full. Oliver took one last breath of air and started to kick the driver's side window. He anticipated that his efforts to get out of the car would take some time but the window popped out of its frame like it was a piece of paper. He started wiggling himself out of the window as the car sunk deeper. By the time he was almost completely out of the car, the car had sunk so far down that he could not see the surface of the water.

He could barely see in front of him and knew he didn't have much time before he would run out of air. As he was pulling his left leg out of the car it got caught in the seat belt. He tried to wiggle it loose, but it felt as if it was only getting more tangled. The car was still sinking and he knew it would continue to take him farther away from the surface if he didn't free his leg. He yanked his leg and to his astonishment, the seatbelt broke. He was free. Oliver briefly had an inquiring thought. How could he have broken a seatbelt that was built to hold a person in place in the event of a car accident? Darkness was all around him but he felt a peace that he had never felt before.

Oliver couldn't see anything around him with his eyes, but he still had a clear understanding of his surroundings. It was almost as if he didn't need his eyes to see at all. He could sense a school of fish swimming around him. It almost seemed like they were just watching him to see what he would do next.

There was a large object moving towards him. Oliver couldn't make it out, but he knew from its size that it couldn't be a fish. It moved with an effortless fluency and speed that was astonishing. As he was wondering what this sea creature could be, he then realized that it was coming directly at him. He turned to try and swim towards the surface but it was too late. It was right upon him and he knew he could not get away.

Oliver was kicking his feet as fast as he could but he could not match the speed of this sea creature. The sea creature was finally close enough for Oliver to see that it was a gigantic shark. He let out a scream but of course, no one could hear him. The shark was headed for his legs and he thought he might have a chance to kick it if his timing was perfect. If his timing wasn't perfect, Oliver knew the alternative would be the loss of his leg and inevitably his life. All of a sudden he realized that the shark was not there to attack him. Almost instinctively he knew that the shark meant him no harm.

The shark moved its body underneath him and Oliver had just enough time to grab on to the shark's dorsal fin as the shark began to carry him up towards the surface of the water. Could this shark have come to save him? Could this shark have known he was in trouble? Oliver was moving through the water at an astonishing pace with the shark dragging him along at speeds he had never thought a being could travel under water. It started to get brighter under the water. Could he be getting closer to the surface or was it just his eyes getting adjusted to the darkness of the sea? Oliver could see other fish watching him as the shark continued to travel upwards. Then as Oliver gazed upwards, he could finally see the surface of the lake.

Chapter XXI

Leaders Disappearing

First it was the Middle East that was hit the hardest. One by one, leaders whether good or bad, were disappearing. At first it was just the leaders that were opposed to a western way of life that were disappearing. All of the leaders with a history of oppressing or ruthlessly killing their own people were being exterminated. There were surveys taken in the western world and the percentages were astonishing. The people of the western world agreed with this movement and were behind it wholeheartedly. They rejoiced every time another dictator was assassinated. The Middle East was in turmoil because right or wrong, they had lived under certain accepted rules and regulations, and things were changing.

The only way for the native Arab people to express their feelings was to riot and pillage. So not only were these assassinations tragic, but the countries had become more unstable as a result. The rest of the world didn't seem to be alarmed that these events were taking place. They were just happy to know that every tyrant was either exterminated or had gone into hiding.

Then something more alarming happened. All of the leaders who were fighting for truth and justice, started disappearing. They were significant figures in politically powerful positions. Even the countries that were at peace started having their leaders snatched away from them. It had gotten to a point where no leader or political figure felt safe. It was easy to accept when the people disappearing were tyrants but when the good ones started to vanish it struck terror in the hearts of many.

The vanishings were completely random. There was no way to link the various leaders together. There was no single issue they all believed in that could be considered controversial. There was also, no way to tell who was next.

 The United States president reacted to this threat by making sure he had a virtual army around him at all times. He could not make a move without having at least ten soldiers with him. This was an extreme use of military personnel, but it was a necessary act given the circumstances.

There was one thing that was very peculiar about these events. All of the leaders with red skin didn't seem to worry about their safety. They never made any moves to beef up their security or limit their public speaking engagements. They were spread around the world in different countries, but still had the same nonchalant approach to this major situation.

It was time for the Security Council of the United Nations to step in. Although the head of the Security Council didn't want to make this situation public he had to do something quickly for the sake of the world. A small group of Security Council members met at a secret location to discuss a plan of defense.

Chapter XXII

Only the Strong

Nikhil is meeting with Jeremiah for coffee as they often did early in the morning. They usually arrived at the coffee house as soon as it opened so they could get the first brew and have the ability to talk freely before the crowd started to come in.

Nikhil begins the conversation. "They don't understand us! I think they are trying to make our kind extinct."

"Why are we hiding our abilities? Jeremiah responds with a frustrated tone. Why don't we just let them know?"

"Because they are afraid of everything about

us. They won't admit it but they already see us as a threat to mankind."

"They are afraid," Jeremiah says. "But if they knew more; if they had more insight in our abilities, they would back down."

"No, that's not the case," Nikhil says. "If they knew more they would try even harder to eliminate us."

"For years we have existed among them in peace and harmony," Jeremiah explains. "Why should it be any different now?"

Nikhil responds. "Because they are not treating us like allies, they are treating us as outcasts."

"We have prominent figures in their society," pleads Jeremiah. "We have leaders that are important to their civilization. We are all one."

"No, we are not all one," Nikhil says emphatically. "We are not the same. We are superior. As soon as we start acting that way then we will be accepted. They will not accept us because people reject what they don't understand."

Nikhil continues. "Do any of us understand why we are different? Do any of us fully understand what we are capable of? There are stories of people like us running at the speeds of a cheetah. There are stories of us accomplishing feats that defy physics. Have any of us pushed ourselves to the limit? We have decided to be bound by the rules of the human body. We think of ourselves as their equal but we are not. We are on a higher level, both mentally and physically. We don't look like them, act like them or think like them."

"What do you propose we do?" Jeremiah asks with conviction. "Should we separate ourselves from society? We will be treated like an enemy and hunted down or oppressed. Is that the future you want? Do you want to live your life running as our kind is being wiped out one by one?"

"No, I am suggesting we take on the role of the hunter," Nikhil says. "They are either with us or against us; if they are against us they must be destroyed."

"You are talking about going to war against mankind," Jeremiah says.

"If that is what it takes?" Nikhil responds with anger in his voice. "The Bible says the meek will inherit the earth, but in all forms of evolution it comes down to the weak and the strong. Bottom line, only the strong will survive."

Chapter XXIII

Following

Today was a good day. Samir had a big presentation on a new product that would change the way all citizens would identify themselves.

Earlier, Samir was in the board room addressing the executive council which was made up of prominent members of the government, the heads of all of the major banks and fellow businessmen in the country.

"Instead of having to carry a driver's license now people would have their identity validated through their finger prints. Not only could their identities be captured through simply touching a screen but you could also tie their identities to their bank account. If this technology was implemented, there would be a new way to distribute currency. No more paper money. No more checks. There would be no need for passports to travel. No more signing your name to go along with your credit card purchase. A person could do it all with a simple touch of a screen. Identity theft would be a thing of the past."

Many members of the executive council were excited and wanted to know if this was a real technology and if it could be as revolutionary as they anticipated. The implications were boundless.

This technology that Samir had presented was groundbreaking but not everyone thought it was a great idea. News of his work had been leaked to the public a year ago and there were many that opposed such technology. Some experts thought that too much information would be revealed and it would violate privacy issues.

Samir thought this small group of experts were closed minded and just could not embrace the future. They were afraid of change. They were living in an old antiquated world that was going to pass them by like they were a relic in a museum. These were the people who motivated him because they were the naysayers. They didn't matter in the whole scheme of things and eventually they would be forced to comply.

Later that afternoon, Samir left his office to head home. It was early fall but there was a peak of sun still on the horizon.

As Samir was leaving his office, he saw a man wearing a hat and trench coat across the street from the building. This was not a strange site in London where almost all of the men wore hats and trench coats. What made this man stand out was not the fact that he had a coat on but the fact that it was unseasonably warm outside.

Samir's car was in a parking structure about three blocks away and it usually took him about five minutes to walk there. Samir had a bit of sweat on his brow from walking from his office to his car in a suit. Samir thought if he was sweating on the short walk to the car, that man had to be burning up in his trench coat. It was odd, but he had seen odder things in the past so it was no big deal.

When he reached his car he got in, put his seat belt on, settled his belongings on the seat

next to him and made sure the BBC was playing on the radio.

Samir started his engine and as he was ad-
justing his rear view mirror he noticed another man in a trench coat and hat in the distance behind his car. The man seemed to be
looking at Samir through the back window of
his car. Could it be the same man he saw
leaving his building or could there be two
men who obviously have no clue that it was
far too warm to be wearing a coat and hat? As
he backed out of his parking space and drove
off heading home, he started to enjoy the fact
that he felt warm in the car. It had been
rather cold most of the summer, so a nice day
was definitely welcome. Samir loved his car;
he had always wanted a two-door sports car
and finally last year splurged and bought one
for himself. He had the sun roof down so he
could take in the fresh air. As Samir was leav-

ing the business district where he worked, there were many people around. It seemed like the rest of the city was out enjoying the warm day. There was a buzz around town as if people knew that there would not be many days like this and they wanted to take full advantage of it.

As Samir was heading towards the freeway, he approached a street light that he knew he had to pass through quickly. Otherwise he'd be waiting forever to get another green light. Samir thought it was the longest light in the city. There was always the same homeless guy on the corner who, because the light was so long, would always have time to walk through traffic to ask for a bit of change. Samir didn't like the fact that people would come up to his car and ask for money but he understood. Good jobs were hard to come by and in some ways he felt this man's pain. At times Samir would save some of his lunch to give to the guy to eat. Samir didn't believe in giving money because he was always a little skeptical about where the money was going. When he didn't have food. Samir would just keep his head down and try to not make eye contact.

Samir let out a sigh when he saw the light turn yellow and he inevitably was going to have to stop. As he sat at the light he noticed that something about this evening was different. He didn't see the man and wondered if he had moved to a different corner or perhaps he finally had found a job. Then as he looked up he saw a man standing on the corner. The man was wearing a trench coat and a hat. Could it be the same man he saw as he left the building? Could it be the same man that he saw in his rear view mirror as he drove off? It couldn't be. His office was at least four miles away and no one could walk as fast as he was driving. There was something familiar about this guy however and Samir began to wonder.

The light finally changed and Samir made his way to the freeway heading home. Traffic was normally fairly heavy at this time but today is was light. He was flying down the freeway and would make it home in no time if the traffic was moving this fast. He pulled off the freeway and was heading through a neighborhood towards his home. At this point, he was only five minutes from home.

His neighborhood was like a big demographic soup. It was home to many different cultures and people from across the globe. One of the main draws of this neighborhood was its diversity. There were other neighborhoods across town that were not as safe but in this one; residents looked after each other and took pride in the fact that their kids could play outside on the block without any worries.

Many of the homes were connected and resembled row houses that stretched for entire blocks. The streets were immaculate and lined with beautiful tall trees that cast shadows on the buildings during sunny days. It was a neighborhood where Londoners dreamed of living.

As Samir turned his car left around a corner to head down his block, he glanced to the right and saw what he could have sworn was that same man in the hat and trench coat standing on the side of the road. Samir had a weird feeling that this man was following him, but how could he be. He saw the man back in the city on foot and there was no way he could have covered that much ground. With that said he was still a bit nervous. He got to his block and saw a man in the distance close to his house. Could it be the same man?

It was.

He drove slowly past his building so he could get a closer look at this man's face. He could tell the man was about six-feet tall and had a slender build. Then Samir finally saw his face. His skin had a red tone to it and he was smiling looking directly at him, straight into his eyes. Samir kept driving. He thought about calling the city police but what would he say. How would he explain that a man had been following him seemingly on foot for about thirty miles as he drove home?

The man disappeared from his rearview mirror, but Samir couldn't tell where he had gone. All of a sudden, the man was standing in the middle of the street right in front of his car. He slammed on the brakes and swerved to avoid hitting him. Once the car stopped, the man started to approach him from across the street and Samir felt as if there was someone choking the breath out of him.

Samir always kept a gun in the glove compartment. If this man wanted trouble he would find it, in the way of a 9-milimeter pistol. Samir pointed the gun at the man as he was walking towards him.

Samir shouts, "Stop or I'll shoot!"

The man continued to approach him. Samir pulled the trigger but the safety was still on. The man kept coming so he fumbled to switch the safety off. He fired a warning shot towards him. The man did not flinch and continued to walk towards Samir.

Now Samir's heart was beating as fast as the wings of a humming bird and he fired five rounds directly at the man. There is no way Samir could have missed him but the man continued to come towards him as Samir struggled in his car. As the man got closer, Samir again started to feel a choking sensation and felt as if he could not breathe. It was like the sensation of drowning. He staggered out of his car, gasping for air, but there was none to breath. He fell to his knees on the street and the last thing he saw was the man's red hand reaching towards him.

Chapter XXIV

Taking Over

Cameron and Nikhil are at a table in the back of a restaurant having a heated discussion.

"They are inferior in every way." Nikhil exclaims to Cameron. "Why do you hold yourself back? Why do you pretend that you are average? So you don't intimidate them? Your power is to be worshiped not subdued. You have known this since you were a child. You are better. They are not your equal."

Cameron was no stranger to controversial conversations with Nikhil. They have been discussing their place in society since they met in college. They had both openly strug-gled with how they thought their destiny would unfold.

"What are you suggesting?" Cameron says as he lights up a cigar. "Getting a group of people like us and taking over this land? Conquering cities like the ancient Romans? Even if that was a remote thought in my mind. A small group of great warriors could win small fights but ultimately we would lose the battle. It's the stuff legends are made of, but there is never a happy ending. We are not even one percent of the population. Not enough to even make a dent in sheer numbers. It would be impossible to win."

"Would it?" Nikhil asks with a grin. "Who are the top scientists working on nuclear warfare? Who are the top military strategists? Who are the top weapons developers and marksmen? Who is the vice president?"

Nikhil continues. "To assemble an army would be easier than you could ever imagine. Do you think others have not had these thoughts in their minds? They have all thought this. They know they are superior to the other human beings. They don't know why they have suppressed their abilities just to fit in. They don't know why they have not banded together over the years.

If you are like us, you are taught from a young age that you are different, not just by looks alone. We don't need anything else to separate you from the general public. You haven't been in *one* class where you were not smarter than the teacher. You haven't played on *one* team where you weren't the best player? You haven't been in single tight situation where you couldn't think of at least five scenarios that would get you out of trouble.

We are different in a wonderful way. We have the gift of being superior to men. Not quite a god, but by definition, so close it's scary. Eventually there will be a time when we will be treated as we deserve to be treated."

"You are overcome with delusions of grandeur Nikhil," Cameron says as he takes a few puffs of his cigar. "I'm not better than everyone else. Even if I am stronger, faster, smarter than most, that's not a reason to go out and conquer those who are weaker. That's a bully mentality. It's not a civilized way to think."

Nikhil sarcastically responds, "Who are you trying to convince, you or me? You have been oppressed by those who are weaker than you your entire life. You have been made to believe that you should not exploit your talents. You look at your power as a curse. You believe that it's a privilege to live among the general public as an equal.

You are not equal!"

"Have you ever wondered why there are never two of us in one family?" Nikhil asks. "Because there is an unwritten rule against it. If a family has twins or two kids that are like us, they are either separated or terminated. Have you ever wondered why when you run into someone like you, there is something oddly familiar, as if you may have met them before? Well, the answer to that is there is a good chance you *have* met them before, in spirit, because we are all family.

We are not a freak of nature. We are nature correcting itself. We are what nature intended humans to be. Humans are not supposed to be weak in anyway. Humans are not supposed to ever get sick or hurt. Humans are supposed to be the dominant beings on this earth."

"Is that what you think Nikhil?" Cameron asks. "Do you think we are dominant beings on earth, gods among men?"

"Cameron my friend," Nikhil continues. "The only difference we have is, I don't just think it."

Nikhil starts to walk away and says. "Oh yeah...to adequately answer your earlier question, I'm not talking about taking over this land, I am talking about taking over the world."

Chapter XXV

Mission

The task force had been plotting for weeks. They had assembled an operations team of specialists from within their ranks for one mission. Their mission was to find the group that was responsible for executing key members of the order and eliminate every member of the group. They had been tracking this mysterious group across the globe, trying to pinpoint the next place they would surface. They knew this group was dangerous and could be a detriment to the order. Now their number one priority was to find them and execute them all.

One of the members of the group they were tracking was last seen in London. He must have been closing in on the trail of another member of the order. They were frantically trying to find a clue to his whereabouts or whom he was targeting as the next victim. There were many members of the order in London but the one that first came to mind was Stan.

Stan was an integral member of the order. He had held various leadership positions and was currently the treasurer of the order. He was instrumental in helping the order's coffers grow and this coincided with the orders growth in power. Stan knew about his colleagues who had been killed and feared for his life.

Stan would walk around the streets of London with two body guards with him at all times. He knew his days were numbered. There was always a feeling that someone was watching him and in reality there was.

It was only a matter of time before Stan was finally face to face with the assailant who had disposed of his bodyguards in seconds. Stan was overcome with an eerie familiarity about the assailant. By the time the task force arrived in London to come to Stan's aid, it was too late.

Another key member of the order was gone. There was no system to the killings. Members were disappearing one-by-one with no sequence or indication of who would be next. The task force had sent out a message to all of the members to be on the lookout. If there were any leads to the whereabouts of this threat, the order would hunt them down and attack with no mercy. The order had already lost three key members of its the board of directors. They remaining members were subsequently on the verge of all out panic.

Royal Tanor was the highest-ranking member of the order. He was the leader of the task force and a master strategist.

Tanor says to the members of the task force, "One of our most intelligent members has finally successfully tracked one of our killers, but unfortunately by the time we reacted, it was too late to stop him."

The members of the task force had been in the room for two days now, watching the news and trying to send alerts to all of the members of the order. But it is almost impossible to watch out for something when you have no idea of what it could be. They could only hope that this menace would slip and there would be an end this terror.

"We are planning a trip to the West Indies to see if there are any clues that could identify our assailants or maybe uncover what their next move might be." Tanor said.

Samuel, one of the members of the order, was on vacation in the West Indies. The task force was desperately trying to reach him, but he had gone off-line. Their only hope was to send a special team there to protect Samuel against someone or something they had never seen. From the Special Operations military group they sent their best team of men. These five men were skilled in all forms of combat.

One was a sniper. His name was Jack and he was the most skilled shooter in the military. He could hit a target up to two miles away.

The second was skilled in hand-to-hand combat. Marcus never used a weapon. He never had to. He would always use just his hands in combat.

The third was skilled in the martial arts. His name was Mark and was a modern day ninja with all the trickery to go with it. He was especially skilled in stealth maneuvers and the art of spying.

The forth member of the group was their combat strategist. Stephen was able to anticipate the moves of the enemy and he was always just one step ahead.

The last member of the team was an expert navigator. Trip was skilled at driving, flying, sailing, basically any forms of transportation. He was in charge of getting the team anywhere they needed to go.

The team flew to Jamaica to find their colleague and bring him back safely.

They took a private plane to Jamaica and landed in the middle of the night. It was not the rainy season but that night the rain was so heavy you could barely see ten feet in front of you.

They found Samuel quickly and warned him about the potential danger. After they sent Samuel and his family to a secret location off the island, they got a call from the headquarters to just observe the surroundings for a while to see if their enemies would eventually show themselves.

After days of surveillance, Marcus finally got a glimpse of the would be attacker. He was a tall slender man who looked very familiar. The rain was coming down so hard it was tough to make out his face, but Marcus knew they had met in the past. The assailant had two visible weapons. One looked like a modified hand gun and the other was a sharp object of some sort. Marcus had no weapons but that was natural for him as he was skilled in hand-to-hand combat and preferred that method of fighting above anything else. He was too far away to thwart an attack if the man used a gun.

So Marcus yelled towards the man. "if it is my time to die, let it be at the hands of another man, not from a weapon." The assailant obliged and put down his weapons as he approached him. He was playing right into Marcus's hands. Marcus had never met a man who could beat him at his own game. He felt the utmost confidence about this scenario.

The rain was coming down just hard enough that it would help mask the speed of Marcus' hands and feet. Marcus felt this would inevitable be to the detriment of his opponent. As the two men engaged in battle, Marcus noticed that no matter how fast he would strike, his opponent was faster. Marcus felt like his opponent was toying with him and for the first time in his life, Marcus felt like his opponent had the upper hand. Marcus tried a move that had always worked in battle. Fake low and attack the neck with enough force to stop his opponent from breathing. Marcus executed the move flawlessly and struck his opponent's neck with enough force to disintegrate his larynx. It was then that he realized he was not dealing with an ordinary man. His hand felt like he had just punched a brick wall. Out of the corner of his eye, he could see a blow coming from his opponent that would surely end his life.

As Trip was driving, it became quite clear that

he was being followed. Even someone not trained in surveillance would know this. At every turn Trip tried to get a glimpse of who was tailing him, but he could never get a good read on the person. It definitely wasn't the local law enforcement because they had already been notified and were asked to stay away from this team's business. It couldn't be a coincidence that someone happened to be going in the same direction because all of the turns he made were calculated to a point that even if someone were lost, they would not have taken the same path.

The person following him kept the exact amount of distance from his car even as Trip experimented with speeding up and slowing down. Who could it be? Trip knew it couldn't be a native of Jamaica. It wasn't someone looking to potentially try and rob him. Then he had a terrifying feeling. Could this be the person they were sent to find? Could this person be one step ahead of him? Was Trip stalking the potential assailant or was he being stalked?

At that moment Trip decided to lose this person who had been following him. He stepped on the gas and began to speed away. He was a skilled driver, one of the best in the world and could push any vehicle to its limit. The roads were winding and treacherous. It wouldn't be long before he would lose his stalker. Trip made turns that only the most skilled driver could make. He cut through residential areas barely missing obstacles and objects. He drove through highly populated areas causing people to dive out of the way to avoid being hit.

Trip jumped in and out of oncoming traffic causing accidents everywhere, but his stalker was right on his tail, keeping the same distance as he had before. It was like he was trying to drive away from his shadow on a sunny day. Then as he glanced in the mirror, he finally got a glimpse of the driver. He looked familiar. He looked like someone he had seen before but he couldn't remember where.

Then Trip came to a market area where he could not drive anymore. He jumped out of the car and ran through the crowd of people. He did not turn back, but he knew his stalker was right behind him. As he dipped in and out of people he could feel his stalker closing in. Then he saw a man on the corner on a motorcycle. This would be his method of escape. Trip knocked the man off a motorcycle and jumped on. He proceeded to gun it. He went zero to sixty miles per hour in about four seconds and knew he would escape. In his side mirror he could see his assailant chasing him on foot. It was only a matter of time before he would be completely out of range. Then he noticed something, it was something absolutely incredible. His assailant was still right behind him running. As he glanced down at his speedometer he noticed he was going 106 miles per hour. Impossible, he thought. He then felt a hand grab his shoulder as he watched the bike rolling in front of him without him being on it.

Jack had been following the target for about six hours. He was waiting for the right moment to take him out. From a distance he didn't look dangerous. He was a tall, slender man in a coat that was too heavy for the warm weather. The target moved quickly around pedestrians, just fast enough to prevent Jack from having a clear shot and then he would move behind a person or a wall or a pole. It was like he was toying with him to test his skills as a marksman.

Clouds started to roll in and it began to drizzle. The rain would only be a small hindrance and would not affect his shot. Jack had been in situations where there was heavy rain and it never stopped him from getting his shot off and killing his target. The man started to move a bit faster, but Jack knew he was getting close to executing the perfect shot. As Jack kept an eye on the target, he finally saw his face. The man looked familiar, but he couldn't place where he had seen him before.

Jack found a perch where he could set up his gun and got ready to make the shot. He was about five hundred feet south of his target. He knew this was the guy he was after and he got ready to pull the trigger. Jack was an expert sniper and was just as good at positioning himself so the target could not see him.

He was aiming at the man's head so there would be no chance of survival. He pulled the trigger, but something happened that had never happened before. He missed.

Jack quickly took five more shots at him, missing his target each time. How could he have missed? He was firing directly at his target and it was like the bullets were going through him. As he gazed into the scope he noticed the assailant looking directly at him. How could he know where the bullets were coming from and how could he even know Jack was there? Jack had perfectly camouflaged himself in the trees and with the rain coming down, he could not been seen from that far away without an infrared scope. As he focused on the man's head again, he noticed something through the scope. He recognized his target who was by then looking back at him holding what looked like an assault rifle and smiling.

The next day, as Mark entered the courtyard it had started to drizzle. He had been in hiding waiting for the right opportunity to show himself. Because of his skill as a ninja he had been virtually invisible to any passerby. He had been following the target for only a few minutes and it was time to engage in battle. Mark's preferred method of battle was with a sword. Mark had been trained in an ancient form of martial arts that focused on the sword and when this form is mastered, the sword could even cut through bullets.

It started to rain and his target was standing across the courtyard, wielding a sword. It was as if he knew that the sword was Mark's preferred weapon and wanted to beat him at his best. Mark moved quickly into attack formation. The swords collided and sparks flew

every time the swords clashed. Mark soon realized that his target was faster than him, that
the target seemed to be able to anticipate his
every move. Then, to Mark's surprise, he felt
something he had never felt before. A sword
plunging through his heart.

After learning about his partner's fate,
Stephen thought of several scenarios.
Stephen was normally on offence, but he
knew he needed to be on the defensive now.
This was a unique situation. Stephen didn't
know what he was up against. How could one
person single-handedly take out a strike force
that was powerful and skilled enough to de-
stroy an army? How could one person individually beat each team member at what they
did best? He was up against a foe that was
superior to anything he had ever encoun-
tered.

It seemed like attacking the assailant would be what was expected. All of his partners had tried that approach and had failed. Stephen decided to let his assailant come to him and he would be ready for anything.

To speed the process up Stephen decided to make himself visible. He went around town asking questions and showing pictures of this would-be opponent. He tried to make as much noise on the island as possible so that his intentions would be obvious. He left his name and contact information so there was no question of how he could be reached. As he was carrying out his strategy, he was plotting a trap into which he hoped his foe would fall into.

After only a few days, Stephen realized he was being watched and followed. Stephen made moves that seemed careless and obvi-

ous to follow. Stephen wanted his foe to un-
derestimate his skill and ability. This would
hopefully be the edge he needed so he would
eventually have the upper hand against him.

After a few more days of going through the
motions, Stephen started to get the feeling
that his foe was also utilizing the same tac-
tics. His foe would provide him with quick
glimpses of him so he knew he was around,
but he wouldn't make any moves.

On the third day Stephen was sitting having
some coffee at a café and his foe sat down
next to him. He was a tall, slender man with a
red tint to his skin. He could only see his
hands and the lower half of his face but he
knew it was him. They sat together in silence
until the man started to speak.

"Why are you attempting to kill me? The man

asks."

Stephen didn't answer at first because he was getting over the shock of his target being within arms distance of him. Then he answered.

Stephen responds. "You are an enemy to the order and frankly all of mankind."

Then the man smiles and says, "Do you believe that to be true?"

"What I believe is that you are in eminent danger." Stephen says with a sharp tone. "Any thoughts I might have had about your existence as a terror have been confirmed by your actions. You have exterminated all of the members of my team within a couple of days and I know that you have your sights set on me being your next victim."

There was a silence between the two. The silence could only mean one thing. The words that Stephen had spoken were true.

The assassin spoke again after a minute that seemed as if it was a lot longer.
"How would you react if there was a team of men sent to kill you? Would you strategize ways to eliminate your foes?"

Stephen knew the answer to that question. It seemed like he was making the assumption that the two men were more alike than not. He knew the answer but chose not to speak.

The assassin continued. "Do you know why you were sent to try and kill me?"

In truth the only information Stephen had was that this man was public enemy number one. He was looked upon as an enemy so dangerous that the government put together a team of Special Forces to take him out. Regardless of what this man had done in the past or had the potential to do, he was not meant to live.

As they were talking Stephen was thinking of how he could reach for his gun inconspicuously.
As he was thinking this the assailant asked him, "why would you even try to pull out your gun?"

Stephen had a horrible thought. Could the assailant read his mind? How did he know his intentions?

"What makes you think I was looking for a way to pull my gun?" Stephen asks with a confident demeanor, but his mind was racing.

The assassin did not answer the question, he just made another statement.

He said, "your gun still has the safety on it, meaning you would have to pull it out, remove the safety, cock the gun, and then fire. That would take at least five seconds."

This was true. Stephen was kicking himself for not being ready with his gun in position. The assassin then said that he also had a gun with a silencer that was already cocked and pointed at Stephen's heart through his jacket, ready to fire. Stephen knew he was doomed. This might ultimately be the last conversation he would have before his death.

Knowing this, Stephen decided to engage in more conversation.

"How were you able to defeat my team members?"

It started to drizzle a bit. It was just enough for other people in the café to seek refuge inside. The rain drops started to hit him in the face, enough to make him squint. The man seemed unfazed by the rain and in fact rather enjoyed it.

"I defeated your team because they could not see past their mission," the assassin responded with a sort of arrogance. "They did not seek the truth, they were just following orders. When you live by someone else's agenda, you die by that same direction."

This was true. Stephen believed this motto and it was one that he had lived by his entire life.

Chapter XXVI

Red Dot

A beautiful young lady named Mira was going through her normal routine before school. She would stare into the closet to try and find the perfect outfit. She always started with shoes and worked her way up to pants or skirts, shirts and any accessories she could match. She would always check the weather because it had a direct correlation to what she was going to wear. She did all these things the night before so she could sleep in that extra few minutes in the morning. She didn't dread school but she was always apprehensive about going. She never knew what the next day would bring so she wanted to make sure she was prepared for anything.

Every night Mira would pray that the next day would bring her closer to being accepted by her peers. She wanted to blend into her environment and just be like one of the other girls. As she lay down to sleep, she would dream of a world without judgment. She would dream about a world filled with people who looked exactly like her. She liked the dark because in the dark everyone was the same. You couldn't tell one person from another by looks. You had to judge someone by other means like the sound of their voice or their conversation. You would ultimately judge a person from the inside out, not vice versa. Mira had an extraordinary skin that was as red as the clay in the nearby mountains. She was ashamed of it because it made her stand out from her peers.

Mira was smarter than everyone else in class. She could learn and comprehend things just by reading them once. She had learned all of the languages she wanted, English, French, Spanish, and Mandarin. She taught herself to play the piano, and violin. She liked math and had solved numerous equations that math geniuses had been working on for years. They would discount her theories because they thought someone so young could never had come up with these formulas.

Mira was starting the seventh grade yet she was on the same level as a college student. She should have been moved up in school to work with the older gifted students but her parents didn't want her to stand out any more than she already did. The thought of her being in college as a twelve-year old didn't seem like a good move to her parents. So they had her suppress her talents while she was at school. She had to do most of her learning at home or at the library.

Mira didn't know why things came so easy to her. She just knew that she had a talent that the other students didn't. She felt sorry for them even when they would tease her. She knew they didn't understand her talents. So to compensate to their mediocrity, they tried to oppress her. Surprisingly she never harbored any hatred for them.

Mira often thought about what it would be like to be what she thought was a "normal kid", with normal skin and normal skills. She thought life would be much easier for her if she could just blend in. She wouldn't be the smartest person and her classmates wouldn't be threatened by her. She wouldn't stand out in a crowd. One might not even know she was there. It would be as if she was invisible.

Mira often would wear heavy makeup to try and mask her skin color. The kids at school called her "red riding hood" or "red-headed step-child" or "red devil." Mira dealt with these taunts most of her life.

Mira should have been very likable among her peers. She was super smart, witty and was an exceptional athlete. With all of her superior qualities she was still humble and kind. Teachers thought she was the perfect student and coaches fought over the opportunity to coach her. Yet she still felt like an outcast because her peers ridiculed her.

Mira knew she wasn't the only one that was like this. There were other people around the world that had the same attributes. But Mira had no idea what her specific purpose was in life or what the future would bring. What she did know was that although she was different, she was not alone.

20 years later...

Mira met with Deven in an abandon warehouse on 19th street on the east side of town because it was the only place to talk freely. The warehouse was located in an industrial area that was not very desirable. There were homeless people everywhere and the police turned their heads when driving through. The streets were lined with trash. There was glass everywhere from bottles and broken windows. The garbage cans were being used to house fires set by the homeless to keep them warm. The warehouse was dark. The only light coming in was from a few windows lining the top of the building. It had been used for producing metal for cans so there were old conveyer belts everywhere.

Deven was in his late thirties but you couldn't tell. He had an abnormally tough life and his face and body reflected that. He had a full head of gray hair from the time he was 30 and wrinkles of a man twice his age. In parallel with the appearance of someone much older, he was wise beyond his age. Deven was an off-the-carts genius and at one point was considered the smartest man in the world.

His intellect was his biggest gift, but it also was a curse that tormented him throughout his life. He often struggled with the meaning of life and never really placed a value on it. Throughout his live he had lost everything that meant anything to him and was well past being jaded about life. Deven felt like the world should pay for his hardships and he dedicated his life to bringing this to fruition.

Deven and Mira usually met in the south east

corner of the warehouse and sat in the dark as they talked. They never wanted anyone to know they were in the building, let alone that they met there regularly. They had been plotting in this same location for months and recently developed a plan to start a chain of events that would change the world.

"Nervous?" Deven asks Mira although he already had a good idea he knew the answer."

"We started a war," Mira said.

"They started it." Deven fires back with conviction. "We are just going to finish it."

"They know what we are up to...we are exposed," Mira exclaimed.

"By the time they figure it out, they will not have enough numbers to be able to launch a counter attack. We have their leader in captivity. They will crumble without him. You take away the leader and they will be in disarray."

"We have been instrumental in secretly making their leaders disappear but they are still finding ways to get to us." Mira said. "I fear that it's only a matter of time before they figure out who is behind this."

Deven says, "I know how they think. I know how they engage in battle. We have the upper hand and we will crush any hopes they may have to win this battle."

"On the contrary, we have lost many members already," Mira says with a solemn expression on her face. "They were good men and women who were operating undercover and should have never been exposed. Our foes are not stupid. They have a high intelligence and that aids them in their strategy."

"They will never find us," Deven says with confidence. "What's the matter? Why do you have that crazy look on your face?"

Mira had been starring at Deven in a way that he had never seen. She has a look of sheer terror.

Mira says. "You have a red dot on your fore-head."

The next sound they heard was a flurry of bullets piercing an outside window and coming straight at them.

Chapter XXVII

Woods Chase

The chase continued into the woods. The rain was heavy but since it was early spring, the forest was still very maneuverable because the leaves had not begun to fill out the trees. A small group of Army Special Forces had followed him into the woods on motorcycles and on foot. They let the dogs go ahead to help in the chase. Members of the Special Forces believed that they would eventually catch this person. They realized soon into the chase that trying to capture this person on foot would be futile. He was faster than anything they had ever seen. Even the dogs were not able to run him down. He made his way through the woods with the agility of an ape and the speed of a cheetah. The motorcycles could barely keep up as they followed him deeper into the forest. The Special Forces group realized that if they didn't catch him soon; he would get away.

How could a man move so fast? How could this man be eluding the Special Forces who were highly trained to be the best trackers on earth? This man was defying the laws of physics with his speed and with his ability to leap so far in the air that it looked as if he was flying. He was a formidable foe for any hunter with an amazing combination of quick thought, speed and elusiveness. His ability to run through and around trees was mind blowing. He ran over small creeks so fast it looked as if he were walking on water.

Then, at last, the opportunity the Special

Forces were looking for. The dense forest finally opened up and a flat valley with no trees
appeared. This was their chance to use the
motorcycles to catch up. As he was running
through this open area, the riders gunned
their motorcycles. Their speedometers read
sixty miles per hour, seventy, eighty, ninety,
ninety-five, one hundred and five.

"How can anyone run that fast?" Connor asks
his men while in pursuit. "How can any man
out run a motorcycle?"

A few members of the Special Forces group
noticed that up ahead there was another en-
trance to the woods across the field. The man
looked as if he was definitely heading towards
that opening. Once he made it to the opening
it would be almost impossible to catch him.

In the meantime, the Special Forces had

called for reinforcements. A helicopter was on its way. Surely he could not outrun a helicopter on foot. The helicopter came barreling into the area full speed as the man was almost at the opening in the forest. The helicopter open fired at the man. One of the Special Forces had a riffle with a scope fixed on the man and started firing. It was still raining, visibility was poor but these were some of the best marksmen in the world. Judging from the number of the shots, the man should have been hit several times, but there were no signs that he had been touched by the bullets. He just kept running at full speed until finally he disappears into the woods again.

By then the helicopter operator had turned a bright light on him and was in full pursuit. The man was gliding through the woods moving in and out of the trees like a maze. At the speed he was running it seemed impossible that he would not have at least tripped, fallen or grazed a tree which would have slowed him down. The man was running at about seventy-five miles per hour through the woods.

His running style was efficient. Although he was running at a pace faster than any man had ever seen, there was a smooth fluidity to his movements. The local military base officials had warned the Special Forces group that they would see something that did not seem possible. They were warned that this would not be an ordinary mission or task.

What were they dealing with and more importantly, what were they up against?

There was a cliff that dropped off into a river up ahead. The cliff was about a hundred feet high and seemingly the end of the road for the target. The man kept running through the woods at a blistering pace. The Special Forces knew that as soon as he reached the cliff he would be trapped. The team of men in the helicopter fired again and bullets rained down from the sky. Trees were being destroyed in its wake. A member of the Special Forces had a good read on the man, but the bullets that should have stopped him in his tracks, were somehow not hitting him. The cliff drew closer and closer and soon the man would see that there was nowhere left to run.

There was an opening right before the cliffs and the Special Forces were instructed not to bring him back alive so they were shooting to kill. As the man reached the opening by the cliffs, the gunmen in the helicopter knew they would have a clear shot at him. They started firing from the helicopter but still could not hit this person. The man was approaching the cliff at a such a fast pace, he would not have enough time to stop. It became clear that he was going to jump off the cliff. But this would surely be suicide. No one could survive such a jump. The cliffs were just too high and there was nothing but rocks and water below. The man continued running towards the cliff without hesitation, as if he wanted to die.

The man was wearing a black bandanna that covered the top of his head. His clothes were tight fitting, similar to a superhero's outfit. The man had a slender build and was like a blur through the air. As the man continued to get dangerously close to the cliff ,the members of the Special Forces group finally got a glimpse of the man's face. The man had a heavy beard that covered the lower half of his face, but you could see a small portion of his skin. His skin was as rich in color as a mackintosh apple.

The man jumped off the side of the cliff. As the man was falling, the gunmen in the helicopter continued to shoot, knowing at least one of the bullets would eventually make contact. The man was falling awkwardly without much grace. His arms and legs were flailing as he tumbled end over end.

Then at the last minute, the man's body straightened up. His arms opened wide and he started falling head first as if he was diving into the water. The man began to soar like a bird diving to catch a fish. He was instantly in total control and moved through the air as if he was cutting through it like a sharp blade. His arms came together and he erected his body into the perfect diving position. As he entered the water head first he instantly disappeared beneath the surface. No one could have survived such an impact. The helicopter hovered around his point of impact to wait for his body to surface but they never saw it.

Chapter XXVIII

Question

Dane's mind was overloaded with information. Although there was so much to take in, he felt a clarity that he has never felt before. He felt as if his eyes had been opened. His environment and the people within it now looked very different. It was if he had been going through an alternative life that was mostly a lie.

Dane stared at Alethea with a bewildered look and asked, "Who was the guy in the woods?" Alethea responded, "My son you should know who he is. You met him when you were a little boy.

His name is Hezekiah."

About the Author

Daniel Alexander Griffin is also the author of "What's my Motivation?" and "Finding Motivation" which are a collection of motivational quotes that take you through the journey of; mental, attitudinal, physical and spiritual emotions (M.A.P.S.). He is also the author of two children's books "Get Into Action!" (Volume 1 & 2) that are written and designed to aid in the fight against childhood obesity by encouraging children to be active in their everyday lives. He lives in Portland, OR with his wife and two sons.